T0156733

PAPER BOY

PAPER BOY

LUCY LEDOUX

iUniverse, Inc.
Bloomington

Paper Boy

Copyright © 2012 by Lucy LeDoux.

All rights reserved. No part of this book may be used or reproduced by any means, graphic, electronic, or mechanical, including photocopying, recording, taping or by any information storage retrieval system without the written permission of the publisher except in the case of brief quotations embodied in critical articles and reviews.

This is a work of fiction. All of the characters, names, incidents, organizations, and dialogue in this novel are either the products of the author's imagination or are used fictitiously.

iUniverse books may be ordered through booksellers or by contacting:

iUniverse
1663 Liberty Drive
Bloomington, IN 47403
www.iuniverse.com
1-800-Authors (1-800-288-4677)

Because of the dynamic nature of the Internet, any web addresses or links contained in this book may have changed since publication and may no longer be valid. The views expressed in this work are solely those of the author and do not necessarily reflect the views of the publisher, and the publisher hereby disclaims any responsibility for them.

Any people depicted in stock imagery provided by Thinkstock are models, and such images are being used for illustrative purposes only.
Certain stock imagery © Thinkstock.

ISBN: 978-1-4620-5236-3 (sc)
ISBN: 978-1-4620-5238-7 (hc)
ISBN: 978-1-4620-5237-0 (ebk)

Printed in the United States of America

iUniverse rev. date: 02/16/2012

Contents

DEDICATED TO:

J.D. Jones who never got the chance to tell his story,
Cody who always listened and loved to dance with me,
and my wonderful husband Chris who gave me ten days to dream.

Prologue

Ted read the same pages over and over again allowing her spiteful words to shred his heart. Soon, the author would feel her own anguish and his mission of death will leave her as broken hearted as her words left him.

CHAPTER 1

PORTOLA REDWOODS STATE PARK

The bride had tears in her eyes as she gently spread her mother's ashes on the edge of the surf. This had always been her mother's favorite spot on the beach and Janie wanted her mom to be a part of their special day.

Everyone was barefoot and wore beach attire, except for Janie's dad—he insisted on wearing a suit and shoes. He would not be in shorts and flip-flops for his only child's wedding. He had never seen his daughter look so radiant. The sun kissing her hair made Janie look like an angel.

He remembered the day Janie was born and he fell in love for the second time in his life. His first love was his wonderful wife, and now his beautiful baby girl. Janie brought joy into everyone's life. She had a gorgeous smile, adorable dimples, and a contagious laugh. Janie had a heart of gold and her compassion for those less fortunate was admirable.

Janie's dad wished she would have finished college, but understood the tough choice she had to make. Bradley, her husband-to-be, had just graduated from California State University in Chico with a Degree in Business, and they were moving to Los Angeles so he could pursue a master's degree at UCLA. His daughter had been studying to become a nurse and he knew she would make a great one. When his wife was battling ovarian cancer, Janie took a semester off from college to stay home and help take care of her. The doctors warned of the aggressive nature of the cancer, and when his wife died so suddenly he was incredibly thankful that he still had his daughter.

The ceremony ended just as the sun set. Janie threw some daises into the surf, her mom's favorite flower, and they all cried. The newlyweds had a small reception on the beach and then Janie kissed her father goodbye.

"I love you daddy, please don't cry."

He held onto Janie, never wanting to let her go. He hugged his new son-in-law and told Bradley, "Take good care of my baby; she's all I got in this world."

"I will care for her all the rest of my days. Janie is the love of my life," Bradley whispered to his father-in-law.

As the couple walked away, Janie's dad turned and watched the surf. He saw a lone daisy make its way back to the shore. Tears streaming down his face, he felt incredibly alone and sad—even on his daughter's wedding day.

The newlyweds spent the night in a plush hotel, courtesy of Janie's dad, in San Gregorio, and then headed for the Portola Redwoods campground for a night of camping under the protection of the giants before they moved to Los Angeles.

Chapter 2

TED

The juice of the peach ran down his chin as he drove south on the Pacific Coast Highway headed for Coronado Island. Ted remembered back, more than twenty-years ago, when he and his companion snuck a case of peaches across the California border. He told his girlfriend to hide the box of peaches in the back of the camper shell under some sleeping bags. He kept a couple peaches on the dashboard so he wouldn't have to lie to the border guard when asked if they had any fruits or vegetables to declare. He just hated to lie.

The feeling of the peach juice on his hand reminded him of the blood that ran down the young man's neck as Ted surgically slit his throat at the campground. A sly smile crossed his face as he remembered what easy prey the young man had been. Ted stealthily approached him from behind as the man relieved himself in the bushes close to the tent. The only sound made was the whoosh of air that escaped his lungs. No final words, no struggle, no evidence. Ted had returned to his own campsite to burn his bloodied shirt and wash the blood off his gloved right hand. Sporting a new long-sleeved black pullover shirt, which covered his black and gold striking cobra and heart-shaped tattoos, he returned to the young couple's campsite across from his and proceeded with the first phase of his mission.

Ted exited the campground and drove south. He had no remorse about his actions. It wasn't his fault he was a trained killer. His country spent fifteen-years teaching him all the skills he needed to be an assassin. His hands alone were deadly weapons. It was just the luck of the draw that the young man and his new wife had chosen *that* camping spot. Oh, the poor wife. How thoughtful of him to not make the new bride live without the man of her dreams. He pulled his truck onto the shoulder of the road so he could fully enjoy this memory.

3

He quietly moved toward the tent that was left unzipped and crawled in next to the young bride. He knew they were newlyweds because of the writing on the back window of their car, *Just Got Hitched*! Her back was to him and she let out a small sigh as if she was waking up when he settled in beside her. From watching the young couple set up their tent, Ted knew she was a long-legged blonde with a dynamite smile. She was naked in the open sleeping bag and he thought of entering her from behind, but quickly reminded himself—no evidence.

The night was pitch-black, unlike the first night he spent in this campsite. That night there was a brilliant full moon, an amazing display of stars, and a gentle breeze. Tonight it was cloudy with the forecast of rain. As much as he was aroused and desired her Ted knew he had to follow his mission. It took only seconds to snap her neck—just as he'd been taught. He traced her tender youthful body with his gloved hand and then exited the tent.

He zipped the inner shell of the tent shut and secured the outer rain cover to keep the wild animals out, her husband's body might not be so lucky. To cover any tracks he might have left, he swept the ground with a pine bough and returned to his campsite. Ted doused his campfire—after making sure his bloodied shirt was now only ashes.

Before leaving the campground, he stopped at the pay station and paid for two more days for the newlywed's campsite. Ted wanted to make sure they would have plenty of privacy and not be disturbed.

CHAPTER 3

FRANCES

A loud thud against my door awakened me from a deep slumber. I lay there thinking of a dead bird on my porch from hitting the glass window on the screen door. This was such a common occurrence due to all the trees in the yard and how clean the windows were kept in the compound.

It's not really a compound where I live, but the property is surrounded by twelve-foot high concrete walls and a wrought iron gate strong enough to stop a tank. The main house is over three-thousand square feet and is a two-story Tuscan-style villa. On the grounds there is a three-car garage with an apartment on the top. There are orange, lemon and lime trees, and the Missus's favorite flowering bush, the Bougainvillea, can be found skirting the entire villa.

From my bedroom window I can see the beautiful blue waters of the Pacific and just a glimpse of the white sand of Coronado Beach. My best view is off the front porch which gives me a clear view of the Pacific and Point Loma to the north. My two cats, Reba and Chesney, made the trip out to California with me and enjoy spending lazy days in their own lounge chairs basking in the sun.

They aren't the only ones who enjoy this beautiful weather. Living in Colorado our weather was so unpredictable. In my younger days I went snow-skiing every chance I got and now in my fifties, I'm paying for it. My one knee is shot and it forces me to have a distinctive limp—of course if I lost a few pounds that might alleviate some of the pain. I'm not fat, but as my granny used to call me, *pleasantly plump*. I'm a big-boned woman with strong-bodied Polish ancestors on my mom's side. My best qualities are my blue eyes and my high cheekbones that I inherited from my dad's French-Native American roots. I keep my blond hair short so my hair is one less worry in my life. I'm blind as a bat without my glasses. I often joke that I need to put my glasses on before I can hear or even think.

I lay in bed trying to guess how long it will be until the dead bird is cleaned-up by the help—then I remind myself, I am the *help*. Landscaping and the outside care of the villa is my job in return for living in the small one-bedroom apartment over the garage which sits about one-quarter mile from the beach. Not a bad trade-off.

Another perk to my job and residence is that the wealthy retired-couple who own this place have houses on Nantucket Island, in Myrtle Beach, and in Castle Rock which is where I met my future employers. I was working at the Castle Pines Golf Course a couple days a week as a landscaper when the Missus complimented me on the care I showed to the plants and trees. Her husband was off playing golf and we struck up a conversation and she invited me to tea after my shift was finished. I never spoke to her husband, but before they left town, two-days later, I had the keys to my new apartment on Coronado Island.

Looking at the printout of their travel itinerary I knew they would not be back for eight more days, so I could lounge around until I felt like getting my day started. I had a late night of writing and decided to stay put for a while longer. The dead bird could wait.

CHAPTER 4

TED

Hiding behind a flowering Bougainvillea bush, Ted watched her front door waiting for it to open. He waited about a half-hour, and when he saw no movement from inside the apartment he entered the main house and went to the kitchen for a bite to eat. Ted knew from his daily observations of the villa and garage apartment that when the owners were home the landscaper would rise at 06:30 AM, stretch on her porch, have tea and some fruit then proceed with her gardening until 08:30 AM. At that time, she would then shower—with that sweet smelling coconut body wash and with her wet short-cropped hair walk down to the Bayside Market where she would dine on a fresh muffin and coffee. Oh, so predictable!

Ted had also observed that on days when the villa owners were traveling, she never gardened until later in the day. She would sleep a little later, but would be up fairly early and on her way to Tent City for a vegetarian omelet and green tea in a French press, or to the Sheerwater oceanfront restaurant at the Hotel Del Coronado for a bowl of oatmeal *crème brulee*. She had a different routine when they were gone, but it is not hard to track someone on Coronado when they have no car and always walk to their destinations.

Another thing the military had taught Ted was how to silence alarms and enter a property without detection. This transplanted Tuscan villa was so imposing, but was easier to penetrate than a hooker. He knew the landscaper never entered the main residence and the cook and housekeeper never came to work unless the owners were home.

Ted had overheard the Missus telling her husband, "I don't want to pay the *illegals* unless I have to so they can just stay away unless we are home, and I don't want anyone in our house when we are gone. Even Frances, she would track dirt in from her work outside. You've seen how she never closes her curtains in the apartment, she might come in here and open my blinds and let the sun in."

Ted had free reign of the villa while the owners were spending time in one of their many homes. A detailed travel agenda was always available on their computer—stupid people thought their anniversary was a great password. He also followed their blog to see if any travel plans had changed. Ted often wondered if the owners ever noticed how much food he ate or if they just blamed it on the cook. His mom always noticed how much he ate and when he was a young growing boy she installed locks on the fridge, freezer and cabinets. He would often go to bed hungry and hating his mom. Now, he understood why his dad stayed in the Navy so long.

The sound of a door slamming shut startled him back to his job at hand. He watched through the crack in the blind to see the landscaper pick up what had awakened her earlier, his first clue to her, a day-old San Francisco Chronicle.

CHAPTER 5

FRANCES

Expecting to find another flightless bird, I glanced on the porch, but instead found a newspaper. That was odd, I don't subscribe to the paper and if I want to read one I go to Starbucks or the local bookstore. After relocating to Coronado, I have tried to distance myself from the world outside of my own life.

All my life I've been a failure at maintaining relationships. I called off my first wedding two-weeks before the big day, divorced three husbands in a span of twenty-years, and I'm currently separated from my fourth husband. I have a beautiful daughter, Sophie and two successful stepsons who, after fifteen-years together with their father, have finally started to call me mom. Pete is the middle child and is extremely successful and is a world traveler. Nick, the youngest, has marched to his own drummer and caused his father and me a few sleepless nights.

In regard to Sophie, Nick would lay down his life for her. They have the closest relationship of the kids and have an unbreakable bond that is stronger than if they were actual siblings. Sophie helped Nick through some difficult dilemmas when no one else could reach him. When we were adamant that he stay in college, she helped him decide what his true passion was—he believed it was in the service of his country. Sophie helped him break the news to us and even went with him to the Navy recruiting station.

The only other close relationships I have are my husband, even though we live apart, mom, sister, a girlfriend and Sophie my baby girl. I guess she's not a girl anymore, but a twenty-six year old woman. Sophie and her family live in a small mountain town in Colorado, so we don't see each other that often, but we always chat daily.

As if on cue, my phone rings, I toss the newspaper onto my chaise lounge chair and return inside to answer it. It was the Missus calling from Myrtle Beach. What an odd occurrence, she never phones me.

"Frances, I need you to go into my house, please remove your gloves and shoes, and see if I left my jade ring by the kitchen sink. I might have removed it to apply lotion after rinsing out my coffee cup. I would be so distraught if I lost it. My great-grandfather gave it to my great-grandmother on their fiftieth-anniversary. The code to enter the house is A747L. I thought I left the ring here in Myrtle Beach, but it's not here."

Finally, I got a word in edgewise and asked for the code again. She repeated it and then remembered you need to have a separate servant's code and since I never entered the house I didn't have a code. She gave me the cook's code and I opened the villa's door.

I entered the sacred domain and felt a cold chill crawl down my spine. Everything was so sterile, but I could have sworn I smelled sweat. My stomach had the willies as I walked toward the kitchen. I had the strangest feeling that I was being watched; then it dawned on me that Mister L probably had cameras installed to observe the staff. I wonder if they have cameras outside and know my schedule changes when they are away.

In my bare feet, I walked up to the sink, noticed crumbs on the counter, and saw a beautiful jade ring by the Orange Blossom bottle of lotion. I told the Missus, "Good news, your ring is here. What do you want me to do with it?"

The Missus said, "Frances, did you take off your shoes? Take my priceless ring up the stairs to my bedroom, first door on the right, and place it gently in my gold jewelry tray on my dressing table. Then you may leave." Click.

Before I could tell her I *had* removed my shoes, the phone went dead. I did precisely as I was told, with one exception. I returned downstairs to the kitchen to clean the crumbs off the kitchen counter so they wouldn't blame me for eating in their house, but found that the crumbs were gone.

Chapter 6

TED

She didn't even look at the newspaper! After all the trouble he endured to deliver the newspaper, she just tossed it on the chair. Wait, she's coming back out on the porch, but damn she walked right by the paper, down the stairs, across the lawn and is headed toward the main house.

Watching the landscaper fumble with the door, Ted observed her from the confines of the pantry hoping her presence in the house did not include food. He heard her on the phone and saw her enter the kitchen. The landscaper stopped abruptly and cocked her head his way. Then she approached the sink and said, "Good news . . . ," and turned to leave the kitchen.

She passed so close to Ted that he could have snapped her neck before she knew what hit her, but instead he quietly went to the counter, cleaned his mess and returned to the dark pantry. Ted heard her slowly descend the stairs and watched as she eyeballed everything in the room as if she were looking for cobwebs—then she went to the sink, looked at the counter, shivered and left the house promptly.

He studied her as she returned to the apartment, picked up the newspaper, which had blown across her porch and then stuffed it in the box filled with wood she used in her outside garden fire pit. His nostrils flared and his heart raced as he realized she may not see the front page article about the young newlyweds that were found dead in the Portola Redwoods campground, campsite A-14.

The newspaper article reported that, "They found the young woman inside a tent in her sleeping bag approximately three-days after her neck was broken. Her husband's body was discovered in some bushes a few yards from the tent and his throat had been slit. The deaths are suspicious and authorities request that anyone with information notify the California State Park Peace Officers."

Ted thought that maybe he should call and notify the police and tell them who committed the crimes—and that they were crimes of passion. No, he'll let them do their jobs and see if they'll be able to connect the dots. With that he went to the Missus's bedroom to take a nap, it had been a long drive and he liked the smell of her sheets.

CHAPTER 7

FRANCES

"Hey Martin, I've got to tell you about my weird morning. First I'm awakened by a thud on my door, presumably a misguided bird, but no, it is a day-old newspaper from San Francisco. Then the Missus calls me and actually gives me access to the villa to look for her missing jade ring. I took off my shoes and entered the house. I had the strangest sensation of being watched and then I saw crumbs on the counter and I swear I could smell sweat."

Even though we are separated, he is still my closest friend and confidante. We have such polar opposite interests that we gave each other the gift of following our dreams. The one place we get together and enjoy life is our cabin on thirty-acres in the Sangre de Cristo mountain range in Colorado. He loves to fish and hunt, and I love to write and take photos. He is a huge carnivore who loves his beer, and I'm a vegetarian who has been sober for decades.

In fact, it had been his idea to give me time alone at our cabin to write my first book. The cabin has no electricity, no cell phone service, no running water, quite isolated except for a few cars that drive by on the dirt road about three-hundred yards down the driveway. It is about seven-hundred square feet—perfect for writing and not being disturbed. Martin and I remodeled the interior walls and ceiling with what we call *rescued wood*, which consisted of pine and oak wood slats that we removed from discarded pallets and used them in the interior.

We also removed the suspended ceiling tiles and added a loft bedroom with beautiful Aspen railing that we built ourselves. The cabin is buffeted on the west by scrub oak and a sage-covered ridge. There are spruce and pine trees to the north with amazing cliffs at the top of the ridge. Then we are surrounded by pine trees to the south and east, with an opening in the trees so I can watch the sunset from my porch swing.

So with the beautiful views, plenty of food, tea and my two cats, I settled in for ten-days of *me* time. Martin stayed busy at our home in the outskirts of Castle Rock with our two black labs, Tar Heel and Blue Devil, and our horse Cody. We have always been a *house divided* when it comes to college basketball so we each named one of our dogs after our favorite team. I named the male after North Carolina and he named the female for his beloved Duke University. Martin named our horse after Cody, Wyoming. Tony Bennett may sing about leaving his heart in San Francisco, but Martin definitely left his heart in Wyoming. At times, I feel like my heart is at our cabin where I wrote my first book, *Ten Days to Dream*. It never made the bestseller list, but was a personal tome of insights, memories and opinions about whom or whatever came to my mind.

During my conversation with Martin, he told me, "The newspaper was probably delivered to the wrong address and the crumbs blew off the counter."

He gave such a typical male response. Since he hadn't been out to visit me, he didn't know, other than my description, that I live in a fortress. It would be impossible to throw a newspaper on my porch due to the twelve-foot high walls and how my porch faces the ocean and not the street. If a paper boy could throw the newspaper that high and far, with a wicked curve at the end, then he should be playing in the major leagues. The only other option being that the reclusive neighbors to the west had pitched it at my door, but highly unlikely since the last sighting of them had been ten-weeks ago. Plus, the newspaper was from San Francisco and not San Diego, which is located across the bay, or the local Coronado newspaper. The crumbs still remained a mystery because of how tightly the house is sealed when the owners were gone.

I finally told Martin, "Enough about this drivel; tell me about your latest adventures."

"Well, I've been fishin' almost every other day, smoked some fish and ate the rest, getting things ready for huntin' camp at the cabin, and had Pete out for elk steaks the other night."

Martin and I restored his father's fishing boat last summer and I was glad he could enjoy long lazy days on the lake. As much as I love the man, I was then reminded of why I moved to Coronado.

"Well it sounds like you've got lots on your schedule, so I'll let you go. Love ya."

"Love you too, Frances, and don't worry so much."

I took a deep breath of the warm salt water air, and smiled at the thought that Martin hadn't changed a bit. I then headed for Tent City, a vegetarian omelet and some hot green tea was calling my name.

CHAPTER 8

HOMELESS VET

The icy wind was blowing from the north and the homeless man pulled his collar up around his ears to try and stay warm. Head down, he walked to his usual bench in the park where he sat and watched the days go by after he ate lunch at the shelter. He would be first in line and the last to leave. The people at the Rescue Mission were nice, but not nearly as friendly as the servers at the Marian House. They would actually sit and listen to him tell stories about Vietnam and his heroic exploits as a soldier. Then sadly, he would tell them accounts about arriving home and being spit on by his own countrymen and women.

He never talked about the dreaded night terrors that haunted him and caused him to leave his beautiful wife and children. The Vet would go days without sleeping because he was afraid of closing his eyes. The visions he saw would take him back to the gruesome sights and horrific sounds of death he endured in the jungles of 'Nam.

One night, his wife rolled over in bed and her elbow hit him in the back and he thought he was being attacked by a Vietcong soldier. He almost strangled his wife to death. Then there was the time he fell asleep watching football with his youngest son. A commercial came on for a video game that portrayed a gun battle. The Vet woke up, jumped out of his chair and knocked his son down to the floor to protect him from the assault—breaking his son's arm in the process.

He became moody and depressed due to his lack of sleep. He often worried about what would trigger another traumatic attack. The Vet thought his family would be better-off without him and he considered suicide, but talked himself out of it because he was not a coward. Instead, he left a note to his wife and one for each of his three children and hoped they would understand someday.

He left Louisiana, hitchhiking all the way to southern Colorado, where he had originally been stationed at Fort Carson, it almost felt like home. Ashamed to ask for help, he started his life on the streets and turned to alcohol as a companion—no drugs, just like when he was in Vietnam. Now it was the sweet comfort of liquid amber that eased the pain. He would often take day jobs to feed his drinking habit, panhandle from the tourists, or scavenge for cans to recycle.

That windy day he found himself on the park bench when he thought he'd hit the lottery jackpot. He had been approached by a man, ironically a guy that could be his twin, about the same age, build and height. The man then offered him one-hundred dollars in cash to help move some rock up at his cabin in the mountains.

CHAPTER 9

TED

Ted awoke to the sound of the villa's gate opening and vaulted out of the Missus's bed. With one quick gesture the bed was made with absolutely no creases where he had laid. The military had also taught him how to make a bed tight enough that you could bounce a coin on the covers. He moved to the window and could see the landscaper entering the driveway carrying a small bag of groceries. He knew she only shopped at the Bayside Market and exactly what she bought.

Some days he would follow her just to keep his hunting skills sharp. Once or twice he thought she had spied him, but he was a master of blending into his surroundings. Even at his height he could disappear in an instant. Coronado was very conducive to his escapades, lots of trees, bushes, alleyways and people who really minded their own business.

He watched as she walked to the corner of the garage, up the stairs to her porch, and she then stopped to open her front door. Not even glancing at the tossed-aside newspaper she went inside and closed the door. She did not realize that because of her inattention to the newspaper, Phase Two of his mission was now set in motion.

Ted took a cold shower, and used some of the Missus's body wash so he could fantasize about her on his drive up north to Point Reyes. Even though the Missus was older and too peculiar for his taste, he just couldn't wait until he joined her one night in her bed with the master of the villa tied-up and forced to watch.

After wiping the walls of the shower and sink to remove any residue, he stuffed the towel in his bag and surveyed the room for anything out of place. He looked at the jade ring and figured out how he could use it in the future. He had been trained for years in the business of killing people and had become a master of death, but he enjoyed a little variety from time to time.

Ted reminisced and thought about how he was such a clever guy. Back in Colorado, he had staked-out a local park where transients and homeless men frequented. When he saw the man who could have been his brother, he knew he had hit pay dirt. The body they found was similar in size to Ted, but the raging icy water had smashed the skull and facial features rendering the remains unrecognizable. The corpse's feet were so shredded that they were unidentifiable. The fingers had been ripped off at various lengths, and the authorities decided that they were severed by the rocks and ice. The evidence left behind all pointed to a fall from a cliff into the raging rapids below and that the victim was Ted. It was a mysterious death indeed; but no evidence of foul-play. Now, no one even knew Ted existed and after his mission is complete, everyone will *wish* he didn't exist.

Ted put on a Navy uniform he bought at a local thrift store, and donned his cover. He exited the grounds via the tree next to the house that the landscaper ignored and easily climbed it, dropped onto the neighbor's garage roof, and then hidden from view lowered himself to the ground. Ted then sauntered across the street to where his truck was parked, safe and sound, in an underground parking garage. No one even looked at him twice; a sailor on Coronado would be like a fan at a Broncos game in a Tim Tebow jersey.

CHAPTER 10

FRANCES

Days had gone by since the last time I heard from the Missus about her jade ring, but I knew they would be arriving back home any day now. Mister L would always text me from the airport they were departing from, with the same message every time; *Destination Coronado, ETA 12:07 PM, open your envelope.* The only information that would change is the ETA.

Mister L is such an enigma. He has no personality, never smiles, always looks constipated and has never spoken directly to me. He looked like a walking advertisement for Tommy Hilfiger and kept his gray hair short and sported a pencil-thin moustache. I'm not sure what he did for a living prior to retiring, the Missus never discussed Mister L, but I know he must have been quite successful. The one thing I know for sure about Mister L is that he is addicted to golf.

The Missus on the other hand is eccentric, but very social—except she has never entertained any friends inside her house. If anyone visits, she has me set tables up outside with umbrellas and the cook brings food out to her guests. If her friends need to use the restroom, the Missus had a bathroom installed in the garage for just that purpose. She reminds me of a cross between Angela Lansbury from her days on the TV show, *Murder, She Wrote*, and Julie Andrews in *Mary Poppins*. I'm not really sure why, but I can see traits of both women in the Missus.

I opened my envelope from Mister L to find my latest instructions: *1) Meticulous landscape, 2) Water two-hours before we arrive so the grass and walkway are dry on arrival, 3) Call the cook and housekeeper and tell them our ETA and to open their envelopes.* He is so weird, but to be able to live where I do, free, is worth some of the strange nuances.

Obediently doing my chores, I waved to the household staff as they entered through the main gate. I never really spoke much to the ladies, Rosie the cook and Juanita the housekeeper, but I knew they were cousins and lived together in Imperial Beach. The women rode the bus up the strand to Coronado and were on-call twenty-four hours a day, seven-days a week, unless the owners are out of town, then they are restricted from the premises. They share a room next to the kitchen and are thankful they have a job. Both women are *illegals* from Mexico, but the Missus likes it that way.

One day she told me, "Those girls work cheaper, longer hours and do what they're told unlike American help."

I wondered if I was an exception, then remembered she didn't actually pay me, but did provide me with an awesome place to live. And really, if I was honest with myself, I really don't work that hard at all.

The owners, Mr. and Mrs. Llyzmeikewicz, that's why I refer to them as Mister L and the Missus, don't speak directly to the staff, but communicate by writing-out the daily menus and chores to be completed. Mister L plays golf every day, and the Missus usually stays indoors and does who knows what. Even though three of the four homes they own are by beaches, I've yet to ever see either of them go down to the beach. This is truly a weird, but wonderful place to live. I have my responsibilities which take up a couple hours a day, live for free, and have the ocean for my inspiration and rejuvenation. More than anyone could ask for or deserve.

CHAPTER 11

POINT REYES NATIONAL SEASHORE

"Kristi, you will absolutely love this place. There are these awesome natural ponds created by the surf when the tide is low and the sea deposits a huge variety of aquatic life that gets caught in the ponds until high tide comes in," Ben explained to his latest companion as he had to many girls before on the trip to the coast.

Kristi didn't respond, she just smiled at him and kept playing with the hair on the back of his neck. For the duration of the drive, Ben kept telling Kristi, "Keep your eyes open for bobcats, coyotes, raccoons, deer, elk and maybe even a skunk, and when we get to the shore we might see whales off the coast, seals, or sea lions." Kristi just rolled her eyes.

The two kids were Berkeley students, Ben was studying marine biology and Kristi was a drama/dance major, this semester, who absolutely loved nature and the outdoors, or whatever her current boyfriend was studying. Ben was originally from Austin, Texas, but moved to California to escape his parent's nasty divorce. He was manipulated by his parents and at times felt like a hockey puck being slapped back and forth for their own greedy purposes. Space was the only thing he wanted from his parents.

Kristi was originally from Fulton, Missouri, who chose Berkeley because of its reputation as a party school. She distanced herself from her family who now lived hundreds of miles away in San Bernardino. They wanted her to attend one of the universities closer to their home in southern California, but she convinced them that Berkeley offered the best environment for what she wanted to study.

When Kristi was only thirteen, she had been sexually assaulted by her uncle. He was driving her home after babysitting her cousins and raped Kristi only blocks from her house. She never told a soul. Her uncle had threatened that he would harm her mother, his younger sister, if Kristi ever said a word. So Kristi kept the secret, but never regained her self-worth and found that if she partied and found solace in other men's arms that she could forget her past.

They reached the park just as the storm clouds were building to the west. Kristi told Ben, "I'm not afraid of a little rain, remember I'm from tornado alley and these clouds are nothing to be scared of."

Ben wasn't so sure—he'd much rather go back to the car, actually the backseat of the car and find something to do until the rainstorm ended.

Kristi won that battle and ran ahead to the ponds with her red, yellow and blue-striped beach blanket extended over her head like a parachute. The wind almost tore the blanket from her hands and she laughed heartily as she fought to keep it in her grasp. Ben caught up to Kristi and realized he was falling hard for this quirky, free-spirited girl.

They did some exploring and then as the rain began to pelt their faces, found an area to sit and snuggle under her blanket until the rainstorm subsided. The young couple kissed and fondled, Kristi giggled and then they kissed some more. Ben thought this was his best trip yet bringing a girl to the ponds and Kristi thought she couldn't wait to see Ben naked.

CHAPTER 12

TED

Ted parked his truck in a small vacant lot used for hikers and jogged the two-miles to the visitor's center at the Point Reyes National Seashore. He looked like any other visitor to the park and raised his binoculars to scope-out his next prey for Phase Two of his mission. He had been to the park for the past two-days and no one fit the description he was looking for—either too old, had kids, or obviously not young lovers.

He was feeling like today would be his lucky day and not-so-lucky day for his prey. Ted watched the clouds darken and people scurry to their cars. Ted knew the weather can always be a force in this northern part of California. The rain started coming down and many cars left the parking lot except for one. Ted began walking toward the ponds that held starfish and other creatures from the sea and lo' and behold found just what he was looking for. Glancing around he could see no one in sight. The rain was pouring down and even the view from the ranger station was obliterated by the downpour.

Huddled together under a small multi-colored striped blanket was a young couple laughing in between long kisses. Looking up at the clouds Ted smiled and said, "There must be a God."

Ted circled behind the couple who were completely unaware that this would be their last kiss. Ted stretched out his arms and grabbed both of the young lovers still wrapped in their blanket and flattened them into one of the observation ponds. Using the blanket, he held their heads from behind until they stopped flailing and kicking and he could feel their bodies go limp.

For a brief moment, Ted realized that the military had also taught him this deadly maneuver—it was called, *two birds with one stone*. He shook his head to clear his thoughts and gently picked up the young woman and the blanket and then laid her down upon the wet sandy ground. After that, he lifted the limp body of what appeared to be quite an athletic young man and placed him next to his girlfriend. Ted then ceremoniously took the blanket and wrapped them up so they would be together forever.

Sitting the youngsters up, he was careful to place the bodies far enough away from the surf so the tide could not come in and carry them out to sea. The sand on the edge of the pond, where Ted had smothered the couple in the pooled area, was already filled with water and covered the indentations he had made with their bodies, his knees and feet. He turned and followed his steps away from the ponds careful to only step on rocks so as to leave no trace or evidence. Ted peeled off his soaked gloves and smiled, Phase Two—mission accomplished.

Chapter 13

FRANCES

Life returned to normal at the villa compound. My routine was back to rising early, eating fresh fruit and drinking my green tea, doing my chores and wandering down to the Bayside for coffee and a muffin. During the day I observe people, write and enjoy the beautiful weather outdoors. In the evening, I go to the beach when most of the visitors were gone; and as the sun sets I begin my nightly chat with God.

My daily schedule is so predictable that most people would call it boring—but not me. I can do the same thing every day and eat the same foods day and night; it actually removes a ton of stress and gives me more energy to use on my writing.

I love my time at the Bayside Market. From the deli-café, I always get a fresh muffin and drink way too much coffee. Some days, inspiration for my writing comes from people walking along Orange Avenue, or the shoppers who frequent the health food store. Leaving my half-eaten fresh-baked pecan muffin and empty coffee mug on my sidewalk café table, I run back into the store to use the restroom, "Hey Dottie, when you have a minute, can I get a warm-up on my coffee? Thanks!"

When I return outside to my sidewalk table, my mug is filled to the brim with steaming hot coffee—the best coffee in the world, and there is a newspaper on my table. I stick my head back inside the market and asked Dottie, "Did you give me a paper when you refilled my cup?"

"No," and with her killer smile and quick wit, Dottie said, "Honey, I only deliver coffee, not newspapers."

Forcing a smile I said, "Thanks Dot!"

I closed the door and returned to my outside table. I'm not sure why, but my knees got weak and I sat back down. The sidewalk was void of any people although a few cars did drive by. No one to ask about this mysterious delivery so I turned the paper over and stared at the banner—San Francisco Chronicle.

I tossed the newspaper on the seat next to me like it was infested with spiders, finished my muffin even though I didn't taste it, and nervously chugged my coffee down burning my tongue in the process. As I looked over at the unwanted paper, a headline caught my eye, *Mystery Surrounds Drowning Death of Young Couple*. I picked up the paper to read the story.

The writer explained how, *Two bodies were found at the Point Reyes National Seashore by the viewing ponds, wrapped in a blanket and the autopsy showed that both had died from suffocation, or drowning, due to the salt water that was found in their lungs. There was no sign of a struggle other than slight bruising on their outer biceps and minor scrapes on their knees. The mystery stems from the location of the bodies away from the ponds and shoreline, and their upright sitting position. The authorities have labeled their deaths as suspicious and the victim's friends and families were all being questioned. Anyone visiting the park, on the day in question, is urged to contact the U.S. Park Police on their anonymous Tip-line or the Point Reyes Station Police Department if they saw anything to help solve this mystery.*

How odd is that? How did they drown sitting upright and so far away from the surf? Could they have been sitting by the edge of the ponds and a gust of wind create a surge of the salt water that engulfed them and they breathed it in? Okay, I'm no forensic genius or meteorologist, I'm a writer, so maybe it was a crime of passion and a lover's triangle gone-bad, hey, and maybe I'm on to something for another book. With that incentive, I took my empty coffee mug inside, dropped a dollar in the tip jar, and waved goodbye to Dottie. I cleaned my table off, tossed the Chronicle into the recycle bin, strode back to my apartment, grabbed my writing journal, and left for the beach.

CHAPTER 14

FILIPE

Filipe could not believe his good fortune. He listened to the radio and heard reports about how jobs were hard to find and states passed laws to kick- or keep-out illegal immigrants. He reminded himself to never go to Arizona and thought how lucky he was to have a job, live with his family in America, and work in such a picturesque place. Filipe, along with his wife, two kids, his mother, four sisters, two nephews, and a cousin shared a small house in San Diego and he rode the bus to work every day. He was not paid as much as other janitors or groundskeepers he knew, but his employers paid him weekly in cash since he was an illegal alien.

He hated that term, *illegal alien*; he would be a citizen as soon as they would let him take the test. Both of his children had been born in this country and he was so proud that they were American citizens. He had studied for years for his citizenship test and felt like he knew more about the United States and its history than those *legal* citizens Jay Leno had on his show.

There was one girl Leno asked, "What famous American Patriot said, 'Give me liberty or give me death!'" and she answered, *Tom Brady*. Or there was a guy on the street he asked, "Which George was the first president of the United States?" and the man answered *George Clooney*. C'mon guys, even a Mexican janitor knows the right answers.

Filipe worked six-days a week at a beautiful condominium complex about a block from the beach. He would take his lunch to the beach every day in hopes of seeing the Navy Seals working-out. Their training grounds were a restricted section of the beach and he would fantasize that one-day, when he became a U.S. citizen, he would join the Navy and become a Navy Seal. He knew his family would be so proud of him. They all loved America as much as he did. His precious little daughter was born eight-months ago. His three-year-old son, already showing his patriotism, dressed as a sailor for Halloween.

He wondered if the Navy had a height requirement like some of the rides at Disneyland, *you must be this tall to ride.* Filipe was five-foot-one if he stood up straight. Filipe also thought it was ironic how some states wanted to build walls or pass laws to keep people like him and his family out, but places like Disneyland welcomed everyone in—as long as you had money. What a wonderful, but crazy country.

Chapter 15

TED

Ted was always humored by how his name rhymed with dead. *Camping newlyweds met Ted, now they're dead. Two lovers under a blanket grabbed by Ted; heads in the pond now they're dead.* The second part of his mission was complete. Ted watched as Frances actually read the newspaper story and never once looked over her shoulder through the glass pane into the Bayside Market to see a man watching her—though appearing to study the selection of wines on display. Hmm, a nice red wine should go quite well with a rare steak and salad for dinner tonight. There was just something about the taste of blood.

He toyed with the idea of buying a bottle of wine for the landscaper and leaving it on her doorstep, or maybe even on her kitchen counter since he was familiar with his way into her apartment. But Ted knew she didn't drink alcohol, only tea, coffee and water. How dull. He often wondered how she did it being married to a man who loved his beer and who ate wild game. Her lifestyle as a sober vegetarian, make that a sober *picky* vegetarian, never ceased to amaze him, what a boring existence.

Ted made his purchase, put the change in a container for St. Jude Children's Hospital and made his way back home. His *home* was a one-room janitor's work area located in the back of the underground parking garage of a condominium complex. It was only an eight-unit complex so there were no security cameras in the garage and no one noticed him coming and going. His front door had a sign on it warning intruders that the workroom was an *off-limits crime scene* and *no one was allowed inside.* Ted made sure the authorities misplaced the active file on the murder of an illegal immigrant who unfortunately had come to an untimely death inside this room—guess he should have stayed in Mexico.

The condominium manager could not provide any documentation to the police to identify the victim, since he was an illegal immigrant, other than his first name, Filipe. The janitor was never positively identified due to lack of fingerprints or facial/dental identification. His fingers and head had been surgically removed and were never located, so the investigation was as dead as the former employee.

Ted had resided in his windowless workroom for almost a year now and it had been his first-step in Coronado for planning his ultimate mission. He needed a site close to the villa for his reconnaissance on Frances—the landscaper. Little did she know that his location in the underground parking garage gave him a direct view in and outside of her apartment from the surveillance camera he had mounted next to the Direct TV dish on the side of a second-floor condominium unit.

The condo residents paid little or no attention to each other and seemed to all relish in their anonymity. Since Filipe's death, the management had contracted all their janitorial services to a local company and no one even came close to Ted's *home*. He was also clever enough to drive a white truck with DOD license plates used by government employees that were extremely common on Coronado. He rarely encountered anyone in the garage and no one had ever spoken directly to him. How nice it is to be so invisible in a military town, but then he reminded himself how he was a *ghost* so it made it even easier.

Chapter 16

FRANCES

The gentle breeze and the bright sun relaxed me in a way only the ocean can do. The heady scent of salt water was so invigorating. I focused on the crashing waves and the glistening sand and all was right with the world, until I felt a smack on the side of my head by a wayward Frisbee. Some shirtless young kid came sprinting over as I awaited an apology. He bent over, grabbed the Frisbee, turned and air-mailed it back to his compadre then kicked sand on me as he ran up the beach.

So much for relaxing and writing; I should put that punk in my next book and he could be the first victim—death by choking on a Frisbee. I then opened my journal to the words I scribbled down before I left the apartment, *young lovers wrapped up in a beach blanket will be together for eternity.* Such a tragic and mysterious end to two young lives, sometimes fact *is* stranger than fiction.

Young love was always a tough subject for me to write about—just writing about love made me feel like such a hypocrite. When I gave birth to my baby girl it was instantaneous unconditional love. But when I think about the men, until Martin, in my life I always wonder if I ever knew what love really meant. So it makes it tough, sometimes even hypocritical, to write about young love, old love, or any kind of love.

My first love only lasted a couple weeks and my love interest almost didn't last at all. I was seven and a boy from my second-grade class caught my eye. He was a skinny, blond-haired boy who was missing a top front tooth. We attended school in *the cottages* which were two-miles from the main school building. The cottages were a grouping of three single-level brick duplexes that were used to accommodate first through third-graders. To get to school, I walked along the railroad tracks behind our house for about a quarter-mile, and then down Independence Street (a busy thoroughfare in an expanding suburb of Denver) a half-mile south to the cottages. I noticed Mickey would walk home on the same street, but cross it and go west when I turned east on the tracks.

I set my sights on Mickey, and we became inseparable. There is nothing like second-grade young love. I think we punched each other more in the arm than we talked, and we never ever even thought of kissing. Then after a couple weeks with Mickey, the thrill was over, I was ready for my next conquest. As we walked up Independence Street to go home our separate ways, we stopped on the sidewalk where he would cross the street. These were the days before crossing-guards, crosswalks with blinking lights, or enforced laws that gave pedestrians the right-of-way. As we stood on the sidewalk about to punch each other goodbye, I told Mickey, "We are done."

Mickey started to cry. I felt horrible, but then he rebounded and said, "I'm gonna prove how much I love you."

He dropped his books and jacket, and then walked out into the street and lay down in the path of an oncoming car. The screech of tires was all that I heard. I tried to scream, but no sound came out. I could not look, I knew Mickey was dead. But then I heard a car door open, a lot of shouting, another car door open and when I finally got the nerve to open my eyes, I saw Mickey being lifted off the pavement and then tossed by a man into the front seat of the car and driven away. The death of my first love had been averted.

CHAPTER 17

CATTLEMEN'S TRAIL

The smell of bacon and pancakes met Joe and Sarah as they sat down to a big breakfast at a local café and made sure they ate a ton of carbs before their weekly biking adventure. Each week they would spend one day together doing what they loved most—mountain biking. Sarah hoped Joe would notice her new biking shirt that she spent way too much money on. She knew his favorite color was blue so she bought a light-blue shirt and had already unzipped it so her small cleavage was revealed. Joe *had* noticed and couldn't wait to get back to his place after their bike ride.

Joe worked in a bike shop, Mike's Bikes, in Petaluma, where he sold, rented and repaired bikes. He had dropped-out of high school and moved from Rock Springs, Wyoming, to be closer to the ocean that he loved and to work on bikes. Joe remembered what his grandma used to say to him, "It doesn't matter what you do in this world as long as you are happy and give it the best you have."

Sadly though, he could also hear his father's voice, "Joe you have disgraced our family. You will never be welcomed in my house again. You are dead to me."

Joe just couldn't stand the thought of living in that windy old town and working endless hours like his father and grandfather did before him in the dirty oil fields. Joe's mom secretly wrote to him each week and gave Joe her best friend's address so he could write back without his dad finding out. She was afraid of what Joe's dad would do to her if he knew they were in contact.

The last postcard she received said, "Mom, I've met a girl who loves to bike as much as I do. She is really cute. I wish you could meet her. I'll send you a picture of us next time. Love, hugs and kisses, Joe Joe."

Sarah was really cute and had been voted *most athletic* by her classmates two-years ago in the high school yearbook. She was the third-child out of six-kids, and if she wanted to attend college her dad always said, "You better get an athletic scholarship since you got the least amount of brains outta all my kids."

Even though she was quite athletic, scholarships for volleyball and track were very hard to get unless you also had good grades. She had been trying to save money to go to college, but jobs were scarce and waiting tables did not bring in much of an income. It seemed customers were cutting-back on tips these days and some people even left the restaurant without paying, leaving her to cover their bill. But, on the bright side, Sarah found a guy who had a similar interest in mountain biking and for the past month they worked their schedules so they both had the same day off.

Today they were returning to a trail that was challenging, and provided them with numerous hills to climb and then race down. They loved to chase each other up the hills; Joe would usually let her win because he enjoyed the view.

Chapter 18

TED

How could she not be connecting the dots! Maybe if she would have read the front-page story from the Portola Redwoods, *then* Point Reyes a few light-bulbs would have gone on. From eavesdropping on her phone calls, which he monitored daily via the listening device he hid in her apartment and porch, observing her actions, and reading her most recent entries in her journal, it was clear she was oblivious to his mission.

Ted ran through the list of items he would need for the next phase of his mission: one mountain bike, water bottle, biking shirt and shorts, helmet, gloves and some PowerBars. This part of the mission would be expensive, but well-worth the cost. As usual, he'll pay with cash, dead men don't use credit cards, and one unlucky couple will pay with their lives. He wondered how many more lengthy trips up the coast he would have to take before Frances figured out his pattern of death.

Many years ago, when he rode this trail, his companion about drove him to his first murder. She would not stop complaining about the thunder and lightning. They were at least five-miles from the trailhead when a severe storm rolled-in. With nowhere to find shelter, he told her to suck it up and ride hard, he also told her they couldn't be hit by lightning because of the rubber tires on the bikes. He bent the truth a little, they could be struck, but he didn't really lie—he just hated to lie.

Ted had ridden at least six-miles on the Sonoma County Trail #7, which the locals call Cattlemen's Trail, when he finally heard voices. Ted stopped his bike, disengaged the front wheel, kneeled-down, had his head cocked away from the trail, and looked quizzically at the bike tire when two riders approached.

"Hey man, you need some help?" asked one of the riders.

Quickly, Ted shook his head, said, "No, I have it under control. Have you seen anyone else on the trail?"

"There are two sets of riders behind us, maybe three- or four-miles back."

Ted, never raising his head, said, "I can fix the problem with my wheel, and if not I'll ask the next riders for help."

The two male riders rode away and one later remarked to the other, "What a rude guy, he never thanked us for stopping and he never looked at us. Did you see that great tat on his arm?"

Ted would have been surprised, but also disgusted to find out that the male riders *were* what he was looking for—young lovers.

Ted reattached the front wheel and continued along the trail. Keeping his head down, he barely raised his fingers off the handlebars in response to the middle-aged women's friendly greeting. He was in mission mode knowing that the next bikers may not return alive to the trailhead. This trail is an old cattle trail and very demanding so you must be in great shape to ride it. Ted was hoping that the next riders would fit the description of what he needed for his mission.

The couple riding his way was just that, a young, athletic heterosexual duo actually enjoying the burn of racing up the hill where Ted appeared to be checking his front wheel. Gasping, the young lady asked, "Need some help?"

Ted said, "Yes, it's my first mountain bike ride," under his breath he said *today* so he didn't have to lie, "and I can't seem to get my wheel back on."

The young man said, "You're in luck dude, I work on bikes for a living."

The couple dismounted and grabbed their water bottles before they laid down their bikes. As they stood side-by-side and only a few feet away from the disabled bike, Ted dropped his wheel and with one thrust of each arm, sent the young lovers to their death. He always told everyone that his hands were lethal weapons.

He removed their biking helmets and hung them from their handlebars. Returning the water bottles to their cages, he then placed the girl on her bike and sent her back down the hill and repeated the scenario with the boy. Once they face-planted on the rocky trail, his deadly palm-thrust to their nose would be untraceable. He removed his biking gloves and was pleased he bought the gloves with full-finger coverage so again he would not leave any evidence behind. Ted hated it when someone called him *dude*.

Chapter 19

FRANCES

Martin had a memory like a steel trap—unlike me who can't remember someone's name five-minutes after meeting them or even a punch-line to a short joke. He can recall more about my life than I can. Over the years, I would tell him stories about my past and he seems to have committed them all to memory. There were many things I wished I never told anyone, but with Martin he was so dang easy to talk to that I really have no secrets from him.

So it didn't bother me when he called and said, "Frances, I'm boxing-up some of your personal things to put in storage so I can get this house ready to sell since the market has improved."

"That's fine with me, I brought along anything of real importance to California or I took my cherished items to the cabin."

Martin said, "I came across your old yearbooks from junior high and a note fell out, of course I read it, do you want me to read it to you over the phone for old times' sake?"

"Why not, I need my chuckle for the day."

> *Dear France, You have broke my heart. I am moving to Grand Junction a million miles away from you and now this. You couldn't even tell me in person. You left all the stuffed animals I won you at the Harvest Festival for the past five years on my door step with a note that said we were done. How cruel. You know I have loved you since third grade. Remember at 6th grade camp when we sneaked away and kissed all afternoon? Remember when I told you at the end of the year dance in 8th grade that I couldn't dance so you just sat with me on the bleachers and secretly held my hand. You whispered to me that you would always love me no matter what. No matter what! I*

*can't believe how mean you are to me. Why, why, why? What
I can't believe is how much I love you and will always love you
even if you are MEAN. XXOOXX Clifford.*

There was dead silence on the phone. Martin finally broke the silence
and said, "I thought you needed a chuckle!"

Again, silence. That note brought back a flood of memories from
third- through ninth-grade, but the memory that hit me in the gut was
the last time I ever saw Cliff. He had moved back to our hometown, his
junior year of high school, and we never even spoke a word to each other.
I was a cheerleader and too busy for a guy who didn't play sports, plus I
was involved with a senior, my high school sweetheart.

A year after Cliff returned, and the day after our high school graduation,
I walked to my bank to deposit the checks I had received. I walked because
I was suffering from a wicked hangover and needed to clear my head
after the party my parents threw for me—complete with two kegs of beer.
Those were the good old days when eighteen-year-olds could drink beer
legally, even though I was only seventeen my parents never missed an
opportunity for a party.

Clifford happened to be at the 7-11 across the street from the bank
when I saw him. I instinctively waved; he honked his horn, started his
red Chevy Impala and came right over. We hadn't spoken in years, but he
offered me a ride. "Hey France, can I give you a lift somewhere?"

"I'd love a ride home," my voice sounded foreign to me like I was a
young school girl again.

I caught a glimpse of my reflection in Cliff's side mirror and wondered
if anyone had ever looked, or smelled worse. The drive home was way
too quick. I never realized how much I had missed Cliff; his voice, his
incredible good looks, crooked-smile and the way he called me *France*. We
sat in his car for at least an hour and talked.

"I'm headed for Texas to find work on an oil rig. You should come
with me France. Let's blow this town," he said with such boyish charm.

I was so tempted to say, "Yes, take me to Texas and let's start a new life
away from here and all its trappings." Then I heard a car coming down the
street; a loud purple Cougar, and I knew what my decision would be. Cliff
slowly drove away as I walked toward my future.

CHAPTER 20

TED

Ted could not contain his frustration. How could there not be a newspaper report about the death of two mountain bike riders? He waited one more day in Petaluma to see if his call to the local Argus-Courier newspaper would get someone interested in the story.

He was sitting on the patio of a restaurant where he had eaten breakfast many years ago. He remembered how awful the service had been that day and how his companion slid out of the booth, grabbed the coffee pot and started refilling all the guest's coffee cups. The waitress was much better today and almost to the point of being intrusive. "Are you new in town? Where are you from? Are you traveling alone or is someone going to join you?"

Finally, exasperated, Ted asked the waitress, "Can I get my food to go?"

Ted walked the mile or so back to his truck. He had left the back of the truck open intentionally and hoped the town hooligans would help themselves to his wiped-down, once-used mountain bike. He had burned his other biking items in the campfire the night of his bike ride. His plan had worked, the bike was gone and *sucker* was written in the dirt on the side of the truck. Happy riding to whomever stole the mountain bike—he hoped their bike ride turned out differently than it did for that lovely young couple he met on the trail.

Ted jumped in his truck, stopped at the nearest gas station to fill-up, and grab a newspaper—but the newspapers hadn't been delivered yet. After awhile, he finally saw a white panel van with Petaluma Argus-Courier painted on the side and a picture of a smiling young boy on a bike getting ready to toss a newspaper. As the deliveryman made his way into the gas station, Ted sidled-up to the back of the van and took a free copy—some days he just enjoyed living on the edge of getting caught doing something wrong.

He found a side road so he could exit the highway and rifle through the newspaper and there it was—an article about his latest mission. *Two twenty-year-old mountain bikers met an untimely death at the bottom of a hill on the Sonoma County Trail #7. Their deaths were ruled accidental due to massive head trauma. An anonymous caller mentioned he had seen a couple kids racing by him on their mountain bikes up the side of a hill. The informant did not witness the accident, but as an avid mountain biker wanted to warn others about riding recklessly, and reminded readers about how crashes could sometimes be fatal if you don't wear a helmet.*

Now all he had to do was anonymously deliver an envelope to the local newspaper office and then head south—again. What an easy phase to his mission. Ted opened the Styrofoam container from the restaurant and saw a woman's name and phone number written on the inside of the lid. He laughed to himself that she was definitely not his type, and peacefully ate the cold biscuits and gravy.

Chapter 21

FRANCES

"Martin, answer your damn phone! Does he not understand that even though we are separated he needs to be at my beckon call?" I yelled at myself in the mirror.

I left another message then dialed my daughter, Sophie. Again, sent to voicemail, is there no one just waiting for me to call? What was that my sister had said, "Life is about choices, and you have made your choice, so live your life out in California and we will live ours."

Even though I only have one sibling, we have not always been close. Rivals most of our lives and now polar opposites; she's out to make a difference *in* the world and I'm out to distance myself *from* the world and according to her, my family. My sister, Annie, who I have come to admire, just returned from her third-mission to Kenya where she worked with AIDS orphans. I always contribute generously to her causes, but never felt the urge to travel to lands so far away.

Well, I guess I could call my mom who may or may not answer her phone and make it a trifecta of no one wanting to talk to me. Mom had moved back to our hometown a couple years ago to be closer to the friends she grew-up with and relatives. She has practically lost her eyesight to macular degeneration, but still loves to go shopping at Goodwill, dallies with her potted plants, crochets, makes cards for everyone on her birthday list, and takes walks to the park we used to call *Birdland*. She moved into a rental house owned by her two closest friends who live in the house right behind her. There's a sidewalk that connects the two properties, the owner's sons maintain the house and lawn, so I know she's in good hands even though I'm far away.

Mom answered her phone and before I get a chance to tell her what's been happening in my life she says, "I can't talk right now; your aunt is coming by to pick me up to go play Bingo."

"Bingo! How can you play Bingo with your bad eyesight?"

"Frances, they have these new magnifying sheets you place over the cards and I use my dauber on the glass then wipe it clean for the next game. You need to get out more, love ya, thanks for calling." Click!

Why is no one concerned that a newspaper was sent to me from a small town northeast of San Francisco and to my private post office box which only Martin, Sophie, my publisher, and my mom know about? I do all my banking and correspondence via the Internet and keep the post office box for personal reasons, plus my mom doesn't own a computer and she likes to send me cards in the mail.

I found the Postmaster and asked, "Is there any way to track who sent the newspaper to me?"

He said, "Only if it was registered or certified mail, but the paper had been sent directly to your box from the Petaluma Argus-Courier. No recipient signature required. You might call the paper and see if they can help you."

So, I called the newspaper office and they said, "We received an anonymous typed request, inside a sealed envelope, with enough cash for the paper and postage, and instructions to send one copy, dated August 30, to this post office box number. I thought it a little strange at the time, but didn't think much of it again until you called."

Dumbfounded, I said, "Thank you so much for your time."

I hung-up the phone and tasted the bile rising in my throat and felt the urge to throw-up. Who sent this to me? Why this paper? What was the significance of Northern California newspapers?

I sat on my porch and scoured the newspaper for anything of meaning to me. There was a book fair at the library, cattle auction on Saturday, wedding announcements and local obituaries, and an article on bike safety. The article explained how two young riders crashed their bikes and due to not wearing their helmets sustained fatal head injuries. I tossed the paper in my wood bin and realized it had been years since I rode a bike.

Chapter 22

TED

Dancing was never Ted's forte, but tonight he felt like dancing. He had watched Frances pick up her mail and frantically start calling people on her phone. He also sat in his airless room and watched her pace on her porch then she sat down and read the newspaper front to back. The wait for her to put together the pieces of his deadly puzzle was intoxicating and at the same time unbearable.

If she had only read that first article in the San Francisco Chronicle things would make so much more sense. How many killers would drive so far to commit murders and especially double-murders to prove a point? This woman was so frustratingly dense at times. He was feeling emotionally and physically exhausted.

Ted stretched out on his *new* sleeping bag, courtesy of the dead young man in the Portola Redwoods. There was no furniture in his room except for a folding chair, tool bench, a mini-fridge, hot plate and his surveillance equipment. His current *home* was such a change from his two-thousand square foot house in the lush foothills of the Rockies. Ted missed the smell of the pine trees after a rain storm and the amazing vistas from his deck. He hadn't been back there since he *died* over a year ago. Ted's second wife made out like a bandit from his life insurance policy and remarried only a month after he was officially declared dead.

Maybe Ted would include his widow and her new hubby, even though they weren't *young* lovers, to his mission—add them to his death list. Ted was not even half-way through his mission and the thought of more carnage got him excited all over again. He reminded himself that he was dead, invisible and had never left a shred of evidence on any of his death-capades. If he kept up the good work he would be unstoppable and the authorities would remain clueless. To the naked-eye, none of these murders have a connection, except they were young couples. But they should be making sense to some addled-brained writer in Coronado.

With that, Ted closed his eyes and fell into such a deep sleep he missed Frances's phone calls from Sophie and Martin. He had bugged Frances's apartment and porch to monitor all her calls, but he forgot to check the recorder before he lay down. If he had not lost his hearing in his right ear while in the military, he would have heard the incessant ticking of the tape at its end.

CHAPTER 23

FRANCES

When I finally received calls back from Sophie and Martin, I realized that only Martin would hear my concerns about the latest newspaper mystery. Sophie had enough on her plate with a recent move, finding a job, finishing college, two kids and a husband to worry about my problems. So I explained the events again categorically for Martin and told him of the most recent anomaly, "The newspaper delivery from the Petaluma Argus-Courier arrived in my private post office box!"

Since I knew the dates of the other issues, he recommended, "You should contact the San Francisco Chronicle and request copies of the papers that were on your porch and also the paper that appeared on your table at the Bayside."

Then we both had an, *aha,* moment and simultaneously said, "Check the Internet."

I grabbed my laptop and told Martin, "I'm leaving my apartment and heading to Starbucks. I can use their wifi and grab me a venti chai tea latte."

Martin said, "You'd use any excuse to get a chai tea! I'm already Googling the San Fran Chronicle. Call me when you get to the *Buckstar,* be careful. I love you."

What stopped me dead in my tracks before I left my apartment was when Martin told me to, "be careful and I love you," he never said that to me. Well maybe *I love you*, but not the, *be careful* part.

For hours, Martin and I, via the Internet and our cell phones, scrutinized the two editions of the Chronicle. A few articles stood out, one about a retired school teacher who now volunteers to save the whales, a double-murder that occurred in the Portola Redwoods State Park campground, and a book signing by Hall of Famer George Brett—who just happened to be my all-time favorite baseball player. This article started a fifteen-minute debate between us in regard to who was the greatest baseball player of all time. He stood by his favorite player, Bob Horner, third basemen for the Atlanta Braves.

Then we got back to our task at hand, we looked through the edition that was left on my table. It must have been a slow day for news because the most interesting story was below-the-fold that described the mysterious drowning death of the young couple at Point Reyes National Seashore. The above-the-fold article was about a waterline break in front of Ghirardelli's factory, which triggered my craving for some dark chocolate.

Martin and I made notes of what could possibly relate to me, the retired teacher, George Brett, my love of chocolate and really came up with very little, but it was a start. "Martin, could you Google the Petaluma newspaper that was delivered to my post office box?"

He said, "I'll look it up in the morning. I'm exhausted and going to bed. Be careful Frances. Love you."

I whispered, "Nightie night, love you too." A cold breeze met me at the door as those words from Martin echoed in my head, *be careful.*

CHAPTER 24

OAKLAND A'S GAME

The two nineteen-year-olds didn't even know who the Oakland A's were playing, but Jeff had won tickets on a radio station contest and called Carly to see if she was game. The hot weather that day was not even close to how hot they were for each other. They'd known one another since grade school, but it wasn't until they both showed up at a mutual friend's barbecue, a year after they graduated from high school, that the sparks started flying.

Carly had lost weight in some areas and gained weight in others since graduating and she was sporting cut-off jean shorts and a nothing-left-to-the-imagination bikini top. Jeff, with braces gone and wearing contacts instead of his pop-bottle glasses, was shirtless so he could impress everyone with his six-pack abs. Their eyes met across the backyard and the two transformed teenagers have been inseparable ever since.

Carly mentioned to Jeff as they walked through the turnstile at the gate, "This is our four-month anniversary."

Jeff could care less, but knew if he wanted any action tonight he better act like he did. Jeff said, "Cool!"

All he really was concerned about was a beer, then another and another, but he didn't want to hurt her feelings so he stopped and gave Carly a big kiss. Using their sibling's ID's, Carly's sister was twenty-two and Jeff's brother was twenty-five, they got their hand stamped *21* and the beer-fest began.

They found their seats, right behind the A's dugout and in the top of the seventh-inning when a foul ball almost hit Carly and made Jeff spill his eight-dollar beer, he said, "We're moving."

Carly asked, "How much longer is the game? Do we have to stay for the whole thing?"

Jeff reminded her, "It's baseball, there is no set time it could go on for hours. Besides there is a cash giveaway at the end of the game for all the radio contest winners and I have to be here to win. I need the money."

Carly took a deep breath and thought to herself, *we will all need the money soon.*

They made their way to the upper deck, got another beer and sat down. Jeff wanted to move again because there were too many little kids running around making noise and he was afraid they'd spill his beer. They moved over a couple sections and began their favorite pastime, grab and tease. Jeff secretly hoped they'd be on the jumbo-tron so everyone could see what a hot chick he was with and Carly secretly hoped that Jeff would take the news well that he was going to be a dad.

CHAPTER 25

TED

Wondering how many calls he had missed, Ted listened to the tape and put in a new one. Was she beginning to put the pieces together? Has she started writing a new book on the death of young lovers? Ted often wondered who had the coldest heart, Frances or himself. He had read her first book numerous times and the acrimonious words had inspired him to go on his mission of death.

Just remembering what got him started riled him up enough to go on the fourth phase of his mission. Even though he had already numbered his map, he would mix the sequence up because he felt like a ballgame, a beer and a brat. He selected his next mode of death, slipped them in his pocket, and headed to Oakland.

It was imperative for him to commit the murders in Northern California so he didn't mind the return trip up Highway 5 or the Pacific Coast Highway, but he absolutely hated crossing the Bay Bridge. Ted read in the paper how the bridge was undergoing a *seismic retrofit* adding to the traffic woes currently on the bridge—but at least if there's an earthquake the drivers would be safer. Fourteen-lanes down to seven to four to two-lanes, what nonsense, too much traffic; it is time for two-less people to have to endure this madness.

The attendance at A's games was laughable in comparison to the San Francisco Giants who played right across the bay. Ted easily got a ticket, grabbed a beer and a brat then headed for the third deck. He knew exactly where there was a blind spot for the cameras. There is a curved area in between home plate and the first-base dugout that none of the cameras can get. Even in broad daylight you would need exceptionally strong binoculars from the outfield seats to see up there, but why would fans be looking up here, when hopefully some macho baseball player would be hitting a homerun right at them? Hope they brought a glove.

All Ted needed was a young couple sitting away from the crowd, oh wait, it's an A's game, third deck, there are no crowds—and he needed a homerun. As he sat watching the fans below, he heard a loud noise as a plane flew over the stadium with a banner that said, *Chloe will you marry me?* Ted wondered if the happy couple would like to join him up in the third deck. The baseball game drug on, two-to-one into the sixth-inning, and no homers or young lovers, yet.

Two more innings and Ted was about to call it an aborted mission when a smack and a chuckle jolted him back to life. There, a few rows down, a scantily-clad young woman and a too-big-for-my-clothes young man plopped down, put their beer in the cup holders, and immediately started groping and kissing. Ted became quite aroused as he watched the girl's breasts rise and fall, the top string of her purple thong pop-out of her shorts, and listened to her sweet coy giggle as she stroked the young man's crotch.

Ted slowly got up, stretched, took a good look around, no one closer than two sections and all the fans below them were watching the game, or in one man's case, sleeping. Had the couple not noticed him sitting above them? Is he that invisible or did they just not care if they had an audience? He crept down a few rows, looked around the stands again and then entered the row right behind the sex-craved couple. The sun reflected off the sharp metal pins Ted held in his gloved hands.

It was the bottom of the ninth and the A's were down by a run. As fate would have it, the A's pinch-hitter nailed a solo homerun to tie the game. Just what Ted had waited for, a homerun to divert all attention from the third deck and with the swiftness of a ninja the young couple's hearts had stopped. Ted removed the stick pins and laid the young lady's head on her lover's shoulder.

Mission accomplished and all before the next batter came up to the plate and eventually struck-out. Ted read in the Oakland Tribune the next day that the baseball game went into extra—innings and that two fans were found dead, up in the third deck, possibly from alcohol poisoning and heat exhaustion. The authorities were waiting on autopsy and toxicology results. They were not releasing the young couple's names, but cited their ages as both nineteen.

CHAPTER 26

FRANCES

Not having a television was such a God-send. There had been times in my life when I Tivo'd shows and became obsessed with other people's lives, but now I am taking an active role in my life—or so I thought. Some days I feel selfish, other days lonely, and today I feel manipulated. These crazy newspapers are weird and I hate when I can't figure something out. Just like watching magicians. I get so frustrated when I can't see the sleight-of-hand or decipher their tricky illusions.

I'm back on my normal schedule. The villa owners returned from another trip to Myrtle Beach. My chores were done for the morning so I decided to shake things up a bit and take the ferry over to San Diego to get some writing supplies at my favorite stationery store, Make Good. It's a healthy ten-block walk into the heart of downtown and it takes me right by Petco Park where the Padres play baseball. When Martin taught at the high school, he coached a player that currently plays for the Padres. We attended a Padres game to watch him play on one of our trips out to Coronado to visit our son, Nick, who is in the Navy and at that time was stationed on North Island.

I wondered how many games Nick went to when he lived out here. The Padres would wear camouflaged uniforms on Sundays to support the troops and allowed the servicemen to attend the games for free. Oh Nick, I never thought I'd say this, but I really miss seeing you. We had some tough times, but you've grown into such a fine young man—and so dedicated to our country.

I should go to a Padres game. Martin and I are both huge Colorado Rockies fans and when I lived in Colorado, we never missed a game during the season, at least on TV or the radio. There was nothing like sitting on the porch swing at the cabin and listening to a ballgame on the radio. I have just changed my listening location to my porch in Coronado and listen to my second favorite team the Padres.

My initial connection to Coronado and San Diego was during my college days. I first came to San Diego on a Business Club trip when I was attending Ft. Lewis College in Durango, with my high school sweetheart. We drove from Colorado in his purple Cougar and stayed at Vacation Village up in Mission Bay. One outing took us to SeaWorld where I was chosen out of the audience to be *kissed* by Shamu the Killer Whale. Shamu's tongue was like a slab of liver being slapped against my cheek, and was the most exciting thing I'd ever done in my life.

We also drove to Tijuana, Mexico, which was not recommended by our advisors. While driving the wrong-way down a one-way street, we were stopped by the Federales. Neither of us spoke Spanish, although Anthony could have passed for a Mexican with his dark Italian looks. Anthony guessed that he needed to get out his wallet and registration, like he would in the States. Not saying a word, but smoking a disgusting cigar, the officer tossed the registration back into the car and took the wallet. He looked at Anthony's license then opened-up the wallet and took all his cash. The Mexican policeman threw Anthony's wallet into my lap, blew nasty cigar smoke into the window, turned and walked back to his car, then slowly drove away. As he drove by he looked over at our stunned faces and smiled a toothless grin.

We both sat there in shock. We had been warned numerous times about driving in Mexico or even going to Tijuana, but nothing prepared us for this. So, with a four-foot Mother Mary ceramic yard ornament for Anthony's mom, and velvet Elvis painting for my mom, we sheepishly left Mexico, praying we wouldn't get stopped at the border. I mean really, who would even notice two college kids in a bright purple Cougar with loud exhaust pipes, traveling with the Madre and the King in the backseat?

The last night we were in San Diego, Anthony wanted to take me somewhere special. Thankfully, we had stashed some of our money in our suitcases at the motel so we had a few dollars left to spend, minus the money we would need for gas and food for the trip home. Being college kids in the late 1970s, we didn't have credit cards at our disposal. He drove me over the exquisite Coronado Bay Bridge at night. Being elevated on concrete pillars, the bridge gives you the feeling of flying on a magic carpet with only a few lights to guide you to the other side of the bay. We couldn't afford to eat at the Hotel Del Coronado, so we found a little deli and then walked back to the stunning beach. Here I am, thirty-five years later, on that very same beach where today I sit and write.

CHAPTER 27

TED

With the Oakland Tribune burning a hole in his truck seat, Ted had the pedal to the metal when he heard the sirens. Damn, he knew better than to speed. With his heart racing, Ted reluctantly pulled over and fortunately for Ted, the state trooper kept racing by. Even though he had spent a lot of money to purchase a new ID, it was bound to create some questions if they ran it through the system.

Back on the road, Ted maintained a slower speed and tried to figure out a new way to deliver the news. During the two-years his family was stationed in Jacksonville, Florida, he was a paper boy. He rode his bike and always hit the subscriber's front porch with the newspaper. Ted still had quite a strong arm, but today he needed a new tactic.

Back in Coronado, dressed in his naval uniform, Ted waited for the cook or housekeeper to return from their errands outside the gate to the villa. When Rosie turned the corner and headed his way the act began. Rosie eyeballed the sailor suspiciously and then he turned on the charm.

"Senorita, a woman with blond hair dropped her newspaper up the street and went in this gate. Can you give it to her?" Ted smiled and held out the paper.

Rosie took the paper, nodded her head, said, "Gracias," and then waited until the sailor was at least a block away before opening the gate.

Ted double-backed down an alley, and then hid next to the side of the condominium complex just in time to see Rosie climb the stairs to Frances's front door. She knocked, tapped her foot a few times, and then turned to leave. Half-way down the stairs she stopped as the door opened. Pleasantries were exchanged and Rosie handed Frances the newspaper.

The look on Frances's face was priceless. The tan she had worked so hard on turned white and she stumbled back into the apartment and slammed the door. What is it going to take for her to figure out this puzzle? Will she ever go back to her first book and see what a Pandora's Box it was? Will she be able to live with herself when she sees what carnage was left in her book's wake? Will she even live long enough to figure it all out?

Chapter 28

FRANCES

Tap, tap, tap. The noise at the door made me drop my cup of tea and all I could do was watch it be soaked-up by my latest journal entries. My feet were frozen to the floor. No one ever came to my door. I slowly walked to my side window and peered out to see who was on my porch. I saw Rosie headed back down the stairs so I hurriedly opened the door and greeted her.

"Hola Rosie, como estas? What can I do for you?"

Rosie, in broken English, explained, "A sailor at gate saw you drop paper on street."

I asked her, "What did he look like? Did he have an accent, was he short or tall?"

She replied, "Sun behind him and no see face good. White, tall, sailor. Black hair over ears. American. White gloves."

Rosie turned to leave and said, "When man hand me paper, skin black and gold by sleeve."

"Gracias Rosie. Please come by any time." She almost ran down the stairs and I clumsily fell back into my apartment, slammed then locked my door, and was for once grateful I lived in such a secure compound.

Shaking, I sat down on my couch and removed the rubber band that was around the newspaper and opened it up. It was an Oakland Tribune dated two-days ago. What the hell was going on? First a San Fran newspaper on my porch, then a newspaper on my sidewalk café table, then one delivered to my private post office box, and now hand-delivered by the cook who got it from a mystery sailor. Why up-state newspapers, was it because I was a writer and didn't own a TV so I was not watching the news? What? Why? Who? There were way too many questions and no answers.

My urge to call Martin was replaced with a helpless feeling. I remembered he was going to the Taylor Reservoir for a fishing trip with our oldest son Pete for a few days. No cell reception and he promised he would call me as soon as he returned.

Should I go to the police? What would I tell them? Think Frances—what does all this mean? Again, I read every article in the latest newspaper like I did with the previous papers and came up with an answer, Martin. Only one man knew everything about me, how much I disliked tent camping, my fear of drowning, my disdain for any kind of bike riding, and my love of baseball and George Brett.

It was all becoming quite clear to me. No wonder Martin was so aloof at first when I called him with my concerns. He must have just been humoring me that night when we talked for hours and read each of the newspaper articles. It all fit except the sailor, unless he borrowed one of Nick's uniforms and is here in Coronado and not in Colorado fishing. Why would he do this to me? What if he was trying to frighten me so I'd come back home? Over my dead body Martin!

CHAPTER 29

NAVY YACHT CLUB

Brenda couldn't believe she actually quit her job at the bar so she could be with Sam. Her boss had two steadfast rules in his bar, which was a favorite haunt of the local sailors and Navy Seals located on Orange Avenue in Coronado; 1) no sticky fingers in the till, and 2) no "dating" the customers. It was irritating how he would always make air quotation marks with his fingers when he said "dating." She wouldn't be the first bartender to "date" a customer, but when Sam said he would take care of her, Brenda fell hook, line and sinker for an older man.

Up until now, Sam had considered himself married to the Navy. He had never tied the knot, but was now ready to settle down and maybe even start a family. Over the years he had frequented a bar in Coronado and over a year ago had noticed a very nice young lady that tended bar. He had traveled the world, but found someone very special in his own backyard.

Sam had just retired from the Navy and was actually five-years older than Brenda's dad would be if her dad was still alive. Brenda's dad died seven-years ago when she was sixteen, just a few blocks south of the bar where she worked. He was leaving his job late one night after working a wedding reception at the Hotel Del. He usually worked mornings as a landscaper, but volunteered to work additional hours that night because their family always needed the extra money. Brenda's dad was waiting for the bus to take him back to his home in Chula Vista, when a drunk-driver lost control of his car and killed her dad and injured a waitress who also worked at the reception.

Brenda was devastated by her dad's death and felt responsible, since she was the oldest child, to help her mom raise her five siblings. Her dad did not have a life insurance policy, and the drunk-driver had an expired license and no insurance. The Hotel Del sent a card with their condolences, but no compensation other than his last month's check minus the days he missed work due to his death.

Brenda's mother didn't have a job outside the home, so money was tight and living in the small house with all those young kids was quite tiresome. Brenda didn't see Sam as her *golden ticket* out of the monotonous low-paying life as a bartender and the family bread-winner, but as a chance at a real life with a very nice man, which he was.

She had come to know Sam over the past year. Even when he would be gone for months at a time, he would send her postcards from exotic locations and promised he would take her there someday. They never really dated, but they both felt a strong connection to one another. It wasn't until he told her he was retiring from the Navy and wanted to be with her that they became a couple. For their first official "date" he promised her a sunset cruise in San Diego Bay on his friend's sailboat.

CHAPTER 30

TED

The problem was that too many people visit the first four destinations of his mission. That's why Frances was not freaking-out and so blasé these days on the phone. She has not figured it out. She's a writer; she should be able to see the plot of this unfolding drama by now. Maybe Phase Five of his mission will rattle her cob-webbed brain.

For this phase, all he needed was a couple small pieces of plastic and to take a nice relaxing jog a few miles down the strand to the Fiddler's Cove Marina. When he arrived at the marina, Ted punched in the archaic gate code for the Navy Yacht Club of San Diego, which his dad had shared with him years ago: 12071941. The code had never changed over the years; it was, according to President Franklin D. Roosevelt, "a date which will live in infamy."

With his floppy hat hiding most of his face Ted acted like he owned the place and strolled down to the dock. There he took out a map of the bay and pretended to be planning his next excursion.

Memories engulfed him as he remembered his last sailing adventure with his dad and some family members, but definitely not his mom because she hated the water. Ted had boasted about his sailing prowess, but landed them smack-dab on a sandbar. His dad was furious and it took some extreme measures to get them back out into the bay. Ted's wife had to slide-out on one of the booms to offset some of the weight on the opposite side of the sailboat that was stuck in the sand. Even though she had a fear of heights, Ted *influenced* her to volunteer. That's why today he would go as a passenger and not captain the sailboat.

The day was dragging and people came and went. It was close to sundown when the unfortunate couple finally came waltzing down the dock. The man was well into his forties with a trophy wife/girlfriend draped on his arm. She carried a basket with wine and what looked like cheese and crackers. Ted was glad because he was starving. They walked down to their sailboat and she dropped-off the basket of goodies. The couple then headed to the office where they would file a sailing plan; departure time, destination and return ETA. Ted remembered his dad telling him how the Navy Yacht Club prided itself in accounting for all watercraft that left their dock.

Ted saw his opportunity and sauntered down the wooden-planked gangway, stepped onto the boat and went below to find a good hiding place. Why has this entire mission been so easy? It really hasn't been challenging at all. Can no one match his wits or strength? Just as he was basking in his brilliance, the boat shifted and he knew his guests had arrived.

Miss Polly Perfect with her amazing breasts and tight ass were the first to arrive, and then her old-enough-to-be-her-dad partner was right behind her. They played a little grab and grope then decided to cast-off. Ted could sit all day and watch Polly Perfect bend down again and again. It was so arousing to be a voyeur, but to also know how much power he had over these dimwits.

Finally adrift in the bay, Ted made his way out from behind the cabin privacy curtain. The couple was so busy navigating around buoys and other boats that they never noticed him in the stairwell. Ted could smell the scent of Polly Perfect's perfume and fantasized about tying the old sailor up and letting him watch his trophy girl get it over and over again, but once more he remembered, no evidence.

Just then, the old sailor dropped anchor and a squealing debutante almost ran over Ted as she raced down the stairs. Quickly, he backed behind the curtain and watched heatedly as she stripped naked and lay spread-eagle on the bed waiting for her lover. Her dark auburn hair framed her gorgeous face and her breasts rose and fell with each excited breath. The old sailor who was now grossly naked himself, hopped on top of Miss Polly Perfect and had no sooner penetrated her before Ted became the third-member of the party.

Straddling the sailor's back Ted took out a plastic zip tie and then expertly cut off the naked man's airway. Ted still fantasized about the girl below him. The young woman tried to scream, but made no sound. Her beautiful green eyes were bulging in fear so he did the only humane thing he could do; with one efficient move he snapped her neck to end the terror, and saved himself a zip tie.

Backing off the man's twitching body, Ted surveyed the cabin, went topside, hoisted the anchor, and headed toward the sandbar he remembered from years ago. On his way to the shore, he drank the wine straight out of the bottle, rinsed the bottle out with bay water and wiped the bottle clean—even though he wore gloves. He then devoured the cheese and crackers. Ted was a little light-headed from the wine and giddy with completing his mission as he sailed straight toward the shore. He then firmly landed the sailboat on the sandbar. No one yelled at Ted this time for getting the boat stuck in the sand.

Chapter 31

FRANCES

After I hung-up the phone with Pete, I was furious. It all made sense now. Martin and Pete had cancelled their fishing trip because Pete's boss had a heart attack during the cycling stage of a triathlon and Pete had to run the show while he recovered. Why hadn't Martin called me? Probably because Martin was here, in Coronado, dressed as a sailor delivering newspapers to scare the hell out of me so I would go running back home to him.

The only thing that didn't make sense was the randomness of those newspapers. I would find out when Martin came clean, if he would just call. The villa owners were back home so I stayed on my normal schedule and was just about to finish trimming the sweet smelling Bougainvilleas when a head popped-up over the far wall. Scaring me to death, I regained my composure when I saw that it was Marco the gardener from the house next door. He was cleaning the gutters on the neighbor's garage when he beckoned me over.

He recommended that I trim the lower branches of the tree next to the wall because the branches were too close to the roof of the garage, plus it would be less leaves for him to clean out of the gutters. I concurred and left to retrieve my ladder and chainsaw. I set the ladder up and was ready to start my chainsaw when I heard the breaking news on Marco's radio.

A recently retired naval captain and his female companion were found murdered in their sailboat. The male was killed by strangulation and the female died of a broken neck. The Navy Yacht Club notified authorities that the Daisy Duke did not return at its ETA of twenty-two hundred last night. The boat was located shortly after midnight and was stuck on a sandbar on the southeast tip of the Coronado Municipal Golf Course. Names are being withheld until next of kin is notified.

I scrambled up my ladder to find Marco on his knees praying. When he finished I said, "Nothing like that ever happens out here."

With tears in his eyes he whispered, "It is the work of the devil."

Sickened by the news, I turned on my electric mini-chainsaw and carefully removed the lower branches of the tree. Even with the horrible news of that morning, I had to smile. When I trimmed the tree branches it reminded me of a gift I received one Christmas, my very own man-sized gas-powered chainsaw. Something every woman wants to get under the Christmas tree!

I ran upstairs to shower and change. I usually don't break much of a sweat, but the limbs took their toll on me. As I was tying my shoes my phone rang and I ran across the room to answer it—hoping it would be Martin. Graceful as I am, I tripped on my untied shoelace and belly-flopped on the floor when my phone stopped ringing.

Regaining my dignity, even though no one saw me fall, I checked to see whose call I missed and it said *unknown*. I tried pressing redial and it said this number was not available. Geesh, I almost break my neck to answer a solicitor's call—then thought to myself, breaking a neck was exactly what I planned to do if I saw Martin any time soon.

Chapter 32

FRED

Fred lived in Imperial Beach his entire life. His parents immigrated to America from Tijuana, Mexico, just a few miles away and raised him and his four sisters to be proud Americans. His parents never let them forget their Mexican heritage, but knew that their children would have many more opportunities if born and raised in the United States.

Fred's father, Jose, and mother, Angelica, became U.S. citizens right before he was born in 1937, and shortly thereafter his father went to work for the San Diego County Sanitation District, where Jose never missed a day of work for over forty-five years. One day Jose told Angelica that he was going to retire in three-months at the end of the year and he would take her on a Caribbean cruise—just the two of them.

Excited about her husband's retirement, Angelica said an extra prayer at early mass the next morning after Jose's announcement. Uncharacteristically, Jose was not showered and dressed for work and at the breakfast table when she returned from church. Angelica then went into their bedroom to wake Jose up and found he had died in his sleep. The doctor determined Jose died from a brain aneurism. Angelica lasted only four-months after she lost the love of her life and died of a broken heart.

Fred then took over as the patriarch of the family, but there was little family left to look after. Two of his sisters lived in Miami and owned a dog-grooming business that was extremely lucrative, one other sister married into old-money and lived on a golf course in Palm Springs, and his youngest sister had yet to marry, but practiced law in a high-profile law firm in Los Angeles. She dreamed of becoming a judge someday—she idolized Sonia Sotomayor, the first Hispanic female Supreme Court justice. Fred always told her to *shoot for the stars*! He was also a fan of Sotomayor, even before she became a member of the Supreme Court, after her ruling that ended the 232-day baseball strike of 1994-95—he just loved baseball.

Life was much simpler for Fred than his sisters. He lived in the same house his wife, Maria, and he bought in the late 1950s. The house is small, but functional, only a few blocks from the beach and a couple blocks from downtown Imperial Beach. Fred worked delivering mail on-foot as a postman. Fred and his wife walked everywhere or took the bus, and didn't even own a car.

Fred was a gentle soul who would give you the shirt off his back. He lived a quiet life and donated a large majority of his earnings to the local homeless shelter. He felt blessed to live in the U.S. and spent many hours teaching English to the Mexican immigrants who attended his church.

Sadly, Maria died two-years ago leaving Fred alone and heartbroken. Only about three-months apart, his long-time neighbor also died. His beloved Maria died in a car accident when she was back in Tennessee visiting their only child, who luckily survived the crash. Fred's neighbor died of lung cancer, although she never smoked a day in her life. He thought it might have been from the mothballs she had in every room of her house and even on her yard to keep pests away.

Chapter 33

TED

Ted decided not to deliver one newspaper to Frances with today's top story, but three newspapers; the Coronado Eagle & Journal, the San Diego Union-Tribune, and the weekly Imperial Beach Eagle & Times. One on her doorstep, even though she trimmed his easy-access branches off the tree next to the neighbor's garage, he could bear hug his way up and down the tree; one on her sidewalk café table at the Bayside, and send the weekly IB newspaper to her *private* post office box. One way or another she'll get the message.

The story of the double-murder at the yacht club was all over the airwaves, TV, and the newspapers, "A gruesome murder of an engaged couple . . . the tragic death of a recently retired decorated naval officer and his fiancée . . ."

Ted scoffed at the term *decorated*; they should have seen the *bling* he had on his arm in regard to the buxom babe he was bopping when a simple piece of plastic became his worst nightmare. He wondered who invented that plastic marvel, the zip tie, and if they ever listed *murder weapon* on the side of the container under *uses*?

Ted made his way first to the villa since it was still dark out and quietly placed the early edition of the San Diego Union Tribune on Frances's front porch. He knew his every movement was being watched, but he also knew *they* would never say a word. Even though Frances talked to them every day, he had never heard either cat respond except for a *meow*. Oddly enough, a few hours later when Frances opened her door, she just picked up the paper without theatrics and went back inside.

Then after her routine of chores and a shower, she actually seemed relaxed on her walk to the Bayside, ordered her usual and took a seat outside. Feeling like he might be getting set-up with her nonchalant attitude, he paid five-dollars to a young strung-out skater to drop the paper on her table—with her sitting there. Ted told him not to stop until he was down at the Ferry Landing a few blocks away. The boy never saw his face as Ted had approached the skater from behind while the punk took a leak by the back fence of the store. Two newspapers delivered and one to go.

Ted rented a cruiser bike and looked like a typical islander or a tourist as he rode south, down the strand to Imperial Beach. Thanks to his mom, he hated this town. It always smelled like mothballs and burnt pizza. He took the envelope from his pocket, wiped it down and placed it in the payment drop box at the IB Eagle & Times. Frances wouldn't receive her third paper until Friday since they only published a weekly paper.

As Ted spun around to leave and ride back up the strand, he felt someone standing close to him. He turned and looked down into the eyes of Fred, his parent's next-door neighbor. He had aged a little, but still had that twinkle in his eye and a quick wit.

Fred said, "I cannot believe you are back in IB. After your mother died and you did not come to the funeral I thought something happened to you too."

Ted had no idea his mother had died. He had severed ties with his mom years ago and wondered if his sister sold their parent's house. Ted told Fred, "I was unable to make the services because I was out of the country."

Fred said, "I miss your mother and my wife. My lovely Maria died three-months after your mom. Can you come back to my house for lunch and visit the old neighborhood? It will be nice to have someone to visit with today."

Ted hesitated then said, "Uh okay, lunch sounds good."

He hopped on his bike, and for the first time Ted felt remorse for his next victim.

Chapter 34

FRANCES

Okay Martin, game over. Where exactly are you hiding and how did you ever get that paper on my porch? I was actually getting a little turned-on by all the effort he was going through to win me back, but it was still a little creepy. I think he uses the newspapers because of my writing, but I also think Martin wants to scare me enough so I'll move back home to Colorado. The skater delivering the newspaper was *so* Martin. He hates skaters with their slacker drop-out attitudes and gnarly clothes. I'll just sit here and enjoy my fresh-brewed coffee and my dark chocolate chip and oatmeal muffin and wait for him to call.

Third bite into my muffin, I heard a loud car coming down Orange Avenue, it was a purple El Camino and I found myself back on the beach with Anthony. They say smells or songs can take you back to a place and time, but a loud purple car can do the same. It was that night on Coronado Beach when Anthony proposed to me and I joyfully accepted. It was the end of March during Spring Break and we set our wedding date for July 12. He would be a senior in college and I would receive my associate's degree in Secretarial Science and find a job on campus until he graduated with a Degree in Accounting.

The plans for the wedding were fast and furious and mostly completed by long distance phone calls or letters in the days before cell phones, emails, texts or Skype. The wedding was to be at Saint Mary's Cathedral, his family's church. My family didn't attend church, but the previous Fall I had taken catechism classes and became a member of the Catholic Church. We were to be married by our friend, Father Leo Bonarelli. We loved this man. The three of us would go skiing at Purgatory ski area, eat pizza at Farquarts, drink wine and pray together.

Our moms were busy with the wedding plans for over two-hundred guests when I arrived home at the end of May. Anthony stayed in Durango because he had an internship in the business office at the college. We made cream cheese mints by the thousands; both families were cooking food, his Italian, mine Polish, and freezing the food for the big day. I attended bridal showers and received more gifts than our small on-campus married housing apartment could hold.

Needing a break from all the wedding plans, I went to a fireman's convention in Loveland with my parents. My father had been a volunteer fireman for over twenty-five years. I just turned twenty, had blond hair, blue eyes, and was thin with a great suntan. My parents didn't care if I drank, they were usually the ones handing me my next beer—then it happened. I was introduced to the man who would become my first husband. I knew Chevy (he was named after his dad's favorite carmaker) all my life, but I never remembered him looking so grown-up. Chevy's dad was a fireman alongside my dad, my granddad, uncle, and several cousins. Chevy, was also a fireman, five-years older than me and quite a charmer.

After a few more beers and an invite to his room, I found myself saying things that really weren't true about my fiancé. Maybe subconsciously I didn't want to get married, but this silver-tongued devil had me convinced to call-off my wedding with just one kiss.

A long distance phone call ended my wedding plans with Anthony and a heart could be heard breaking from hundreds of miles away. Gifts were returned from the bridal showers and mints sat in the freezer uneaten. Anthony flew home with Father Leo and we met in a park near his parent's home to discuss why I called-off our wedding two-weeks before the big day, and if we could reconcile. I lied and said I just wasn't ready to get married and yet less than a year later I got married on the worst day of the year, April 15.

CHAPTER 35

TED

Ted rode his rental bike back to Coronado and for the first time in years felt ashamed of something he'd done. He never showed weakness, but the look in Fred's eyes as Ted secured the belt around his neck made his heart ache. Why did Fred have to approach him on the street? What were the chances?

Ted raised his parent's long-time neighbor up on his shoulder and then pulled the rope over the rafters so when he let go, Fred would hang himself. Fred never uttered a word; the shock of what Ted was doing left him mute, but the flow of tears that streamed down his weathered cheeks spoke volumes. Ted fastened the rope to the belt, gently slid Fred off his shoulder and felt the rope go taut. Frances would never read about this death in the newspaper—they normally never reported suicides. Ted found a ladder and propped it up against the rafter next to Fred's limp body and never looked back.

Returning the rented bike, Ted took the alleyways back to the parking garage and listened to the tapes to see if he missed anything. Frances had talked to her mom, Sophie and Pete. She also kept talking to herself about why and how Martin would do this to her. Do what to her? That question was answered soon enough. Ted listened as her phone rang and Frances talked loud enough that he could have stood on the sidewalk outside the villa compound to hear her yelling at Martin.

For five-minutes it was a one-way conversation until Frances realized she was talking to a dead phone. What had she said? She was accusing Martin for the newspapers and trying to scare her into coming back home! Whoa Nellie, she got things all twisted around. How dare she give Marty-boy the credit for *his* mission! Had Frances not put together the pieces of this deadly puzzle? She was good at puzzles and mysteries;

Frances could always figure out the suspenseful movies and novels before they ended.

Then why can she not see what is written out for her in black and white? She has a personal paper boy delivering clues to her doorstep, sidewalk café table, and even her private post office box. Ted decided to leave that night for Phase Six of his mission and if that didn't wake Frances up, he would go straight to Phase Seven and then the final piece—get ready Sophie, Ted's coming for you.

CHAPTER 36

FRANCES

"Martin! Martin!" I yelled into the dead phone.

That bastard hung-up on me! I was so furious I needed some fresh air, so I left the compound and marched to the beach. People on the sidewalk got out of my way and let me pass. I walked to the shoreline and let the cool water comfort my feet and the waves soothe my soul.

I could finally breathe normal and Martin, from a thousand-miles away, must have sensed that because he called me back, "Before you rip my head off, I didn't hang-up on you. I just came down LaVeta Pass on my way home from the cabin, and now I'm back in cell phone range."

What? How could he be on LaVeta Pass when he was here in Coronado delivering newspapers to me? I found a quiet spot to sit down and gather my thoughts and then I began to cry. In between sobs, I said, "Martin, I thought you were the culprit who was sending and delivering the newspapers to me so I'd get scared and come back home."

He said, "I only wish I was that clever to try to scare *you* back home. I'll shave, then clean-up the house and meet you at the airport if you can get on the next flight."

Martin could always make me laugh.

Then the conversation got serious. Again, we tried to outline these strange deliveries and I told him about the latest San Diego newspaper on my doorstep and the one delivered by a skater at the Bayside. Since I thought Martin was behind the newspaper deliveries, I didn't stop or question the skater.

Martin asked me, "Were there any stories that stood-out in the latest paper?"

I told him, "There was a double-murder of an engaged couple at the Navy Yacht Club which is south of here on the strand."

He said, "Was it a young couple like the other reports?"

I replied, "The man was in his late forties and just retired from the Navy, but the young woman was only twenty-three."

Then a light went on. Martin didn't know about the article in the Oakland paper about the young couple who died at the ballpark. I told him, "While you were gone, there was a young couple that died at an Oakland A's game and the authorities originally thought it to be alcohol poisoning. I've been scanning the net daily and reading the newspapers that had been delivered to me. I read where the cause of death was determined to be a small puncture wound to both of their hearts. Someone killed them!"

The words out of Martin's mouth were like music to my ears, "I'm on my way. Meet me where you and I stayed the last time we visited Nick. Tell no one and do not go back to your apartment."

Even though the temperature was still close to seventy-five degrees, I froze in the sand. I literally peed my pants and ran into the waves so no one could see my wet crotch. I had to go back to my apartment to shower, change clothes, grab my purse and laptop, and then get moving. All the lights were out in the villa, so I left a note for the Missus, "I have a family emergency and will return as soon as possible. Frances"

Just as I approached the wrought iron gate to leave the compound, a white truck pulled out of the parking garage across the street. I stepped back in the shadows and from that angle I could barely see the driver, but my heart stopped—I could swear I just saw a ghost.

Chapter 37

TRUCKEE

The couple drove in silence for over an hour. Neither one of them had expected the harsh reception they received from their families when they gathered them all together under the group shelter at Goodnow Park and told them their exciting news—they were married! One of the grandmas fainted, an uncle yelled a profanity-laced slur, and both sets of parents left the covered gazebo and went to the local bar without a word to the newlyweds.

There was only one kind soul who congratulated them; it was Lindsey's cousin LuLu. She hugged and kissed the newlyweds then wished them both her best. She also let them know that the rest of the family would come around, eventually, and all that mattered was their happiness. LuLu also informed the couple that after all her failed relationships the family had disowned her years ago, and made her the brunt of all their jokes. She had told her family they could *kiss her ass* and hadn't spoken to or seen any of them until, at the newlywed's request; she came to the park today. LuLu advised them that their families were all a bunch of morons and told the newlyweds to live their life and leave Manhattan, Kansas, in the rearview mirror. She kissed them both, got in her car and never looked back.

No one else congratulated the couple and they took LuLu's advice and left. Lindsey put an arm around his best friend and lover, and now his spouse and said how hurtful it was to be shunned by those that should love you the most. They headed west and stopped just east of the small town of Drake, Colorado, and set their tent up in a campground next to the Big Thompson River.

Lindsey recalled what had happened July 31, 1976. *This was the site of the worst natural disaster in Colorado history; 145 souls lost their life when a violent rainstorm stalled over the canyon and over ten-inches of rain fell in only a few hours which then sent a wall of water through the canyon returning it to its primordial state. It demolished 141 homes and destroyed 52 businesses. Tales are told that at night you could still hear the screams of the victims that were washed away from where the river flooded.*

However, that night next to the Big Thompson River, the newlyweds were under a canopy of twinkling stars that were shining bright. As they held each other tightly a falling star lit-up the sky and they both secretly made the same wish that they would *live happily ever after.* The couple awoke the next morning to rain and windy conditions; they decided to leave Colorado and see if they could make it to Truckee, California, before nightfall.

Lindsey was an historian that stopped at every historical landmark and now he wanted to visit the site attributed to the Donner Party tragedy. He thought about all the mystery that still surrounded the dreadful events which occurred back in 1846. It would make for a great campsite debate tonight in regard to murder and cannibalism. Rock, named after Rock Hudson by his mom who absolutely adored the famous actor, was a free-lance newspaper columnist in San Francisco and enjoyed writing stories about some of the historical sites that Lindsey was so interested in. Rock had hated his name growing-up until the media revealed a few years back, that the famous actor was gay.

Chapter 38

TED

Ted was immersed in his thoughts about Fred when he exited the parking garage. He noticed Frances's lights were off, but that wasn't unusual for this time of day. He had hours of driving ahead of him to get to the campground in Donner Memorial State Park just south of Truckee.

Thinking about the Donner Party and the tragedy that befell them, Ted wondered what human flesh would taste like. Other than licking a cut or chewing his fingernails he had no clue if humans tasted like chickens. He made himself laugh and continued with his thoughts about the Donner Party and if they used salt and pepper while dining on their cohorts. Ted filled-up his truck with gas, topped-off his thermos with hours-old coffee, paid in cash, slid back in his truck, found a radio station, and figured his next victims had about ten-hours to live.

The sun was rising and burning his eyes until he found his mirrored aviator sunglasses. He always thought he looked cool in these shades even though his wife called him *bug-eyed* when he wore them. He found the gas station/diner/campground just as he'd remembered it. What defines the great outdoors more than a campsite next to a highway and a gas pump. There was also an abandoned putt-putt golf course on the south side of the campground that was now inhabited by tumbleweeds and chipmunks. A few people were moving about and Ted sat on his tailgate and surveyed the campsites.

Some campers were walking around, stretching, or starting outside grills for breakfast and brewing coffee. The fresh-brewed coffee smelled so much better than the mud he was drinking so he tossed it on the ground and spit. The campground had a one-way loop and he decided to walk around to the farthest sites and see if he could get lucky. Earlier he had donned his hat with the fake gray hair sticking out, grabbed his cane and hunched way over to disguise his height and age. He wore a long-sleeved shirt and slid his hands into his latest purchase—a new pair of gloves.

At his last stop for gas, he also switched license plates with a car in the repair lot that had a slip on the windshield that read, *needs new motor.* If someone wrote down the license plate numbers and reported them to the police, he always wanted to see the shock on the real license plate owner's face if the police came to their house and questioned them about a murder they didn't commit.

The furthest campsites in the middle of the loop were much more secluded than the sites closest to the gas station. There were heavily treed sites and some flag-lots off the one-way loop. As luck would have it, he watched two men exit their tents from separate campsites and head for the restroom—double your pleasure, double your fun!

Ted limped into the bathroom behind the two men who were exchanging pleasantries while standing at the urinal. How nice Ted thought, two men greeting one another with their dicks in their hand. Ted used his cane to barricade the door. He shuffled over to the urinal where both men scooted to the side as Ted rudely wedged himself between them. Before they knew what hit them, Ted had karate-chopped them in the throat which collapsed their windpipes. Both men were incapacitated, but not dead—yet.

Wanting to help Frances connect the dots, he took out two zip ties, and finished the job. Excitedly Ted left the restroom, but only after positioning both men in separate stalls with the stall door locked, their feet on the ground with pants pulled-down around each of the dead man's ankles.

Ted chose the first tent he came to and listened outside for any movement. He heard none so he crawled inside. The tent was empty, how'd he miss her, where was she? Looking around it became quite evident that there was no couple, only one sleeping bag, a Coleman lantern, and a dogged-ear Bible.

Quickly Ted exited the tent, zipped it up and walked through the willows that separated the campsites. Cautiously approaching the next site, he noticed movement and moaning in the tent. He crept up to the side of the tent and heard a high-pitched shaky voice, "Lindsey, hurry and come back in . . ."

Ted entered the tent through the unzipped flap and was sickened by what he saw. Another man was laying on his back masturbating, eyes closed, and still moaning for *Lindsey*. The gay man released his penis as Ted let his fists loose on his face. Ted became an enraged animal with punch after punch leaving the man with a face even his mother wouldn't recognize. The man's body kept convulsing and there were only sounds of gurgling as Ted exited the blood splattered tent. He left the man to suffer and die slowly in his own disgusting blood.

CHAPTER 39

FRANCES

Taking Isabella Street to Orange Avenue, I booked it seven-blocks down to Third Street, and entered the Coronado Inn's office. It had been over two-years since Martin and I stayed at the inn when we drove Nick's new Jeep out for him from Colorado. I knew the proprietors well because of my frequent trips to the Bayside Market. I would always wave to the ladies who ran the office or stop and chat with them on my way back from the market. The office sat right next to the sidewalk and the sliding-glass patio doors were always open. The inn had been one of the first motels built after the Hotel Del, was fairly inexpensive, and very quaint.

I explained to Jan, the desk clerk and part-owner, "I need the first room on the east end closest to the street. Also, my husband, Martin, do you remember him, will be joining me tomorrow. If anyone asks about my whereabouts you have not seen me."

There was no security at this site, but I felt safe knowing Martin would be there soon. Jan did not even blink when I asked that she put an alias in her computer when I registered.

Jan said, "Okay honey, I've never seen you before in my life and when that tall good lookin' cowboy gets here I'll make sure you have privacy. Of course I remember him—I never forget a sweet-talkin' man in tight jeans. Yee-haw!" With a wink, a wiggle of her eyebrows and a wicked smile, she handed me my room key—no questions asked.

I entered our room which was directly across from the office. The room had windows on all three-sides. There was a small window that looked directly south down Orange Avenue from the bathroom, a window next to the television that looked east on Third Avenue, and the front window next to the door that allowed me to look north up Orange Avenue and directly into the office. I could see the Bayside Market from the front window and craved a late-night snack, but realized that I won't even risk walking the fifty-yards to get a muffin and coffee in the morning.

Sitting on the edge of the bed, I turned on the television. That was the first time I'd watched TV in months. The eleven o'clock news was on and I watched intently as they updated the story about the recent murders on the sailboat. Nothing really new to report other than they thought it was odd that the bottle of wine at the scene was empty, but the glasses were clean. They sent the bottle to the lab to be dusted for prints or saliva residue. The crime still remained a mystery.

I remembered sailing with my father-in-law, Les, out of that same yacht club years ago. His wife would send us lunch—cold Spam sandwiches on white bread with mustard. Les hated the sandwiches, so on our way home from sailing we would stop at McDonald's and get some *real food* before going home. I smiled when I recalled the look on Sophie's face when she opened a brown paper bag thinking it was part of our lunch and it was actually one of Grandpa Les's Depends that his wife had packed for him. Wow, where did that memory come from?

Turning my attention back to the TV there was a story on how fire inspectors visited a local bakery and found numerous violations of the fire code. Again, the memories flooded in. I had once been married to a fireman; he was the man I kissed at the fireman's convention then married ten-months later. He and I had fun while it lasted. We partied every night unless we were working our part-time job as drapery installers, or remodeling our basement complete with a bar that could sit six people, and always had a keg on tap. There was a poker table, a large-screen projection TV, and a make-you-go-deaf stereo system with a state-of-the-art reel-to-reel tape player. I could still hear Rita Coolidge singing, "Your love is lifting me higher . . . ," ringing in my ears.

This was my first marriage and the casual observer might have thought we were an ideal couple, but we weren't. Too much drinking, plus I had to follow such strict rules and procedures. I guess the term you could use for me during this time of my life was submissive. I would rush home from work, dust and vacuum, clean the bathroom and have dinner fixed every day. When I say vacuum, I mean the wheel-marks of the vacuum had to leave parallel lines in the bright olive-green colored shag carpet.

Same procedure for mowing the lawn; you mowed it once in a circle to cut the grass one way then you went back and made sure the wheels of the mower left straight lines across the yard. It was manicured finer than a golf course—I could have quit my secretarial job at Coors and got hired as a groundskeeper at a ballpark. Also, my husband's towel had to be heated in the morning, even in the summer. I would run downstairs to the basement laundry-room and toss a clean towel in the dryer to warm it up.

After only three-years of marriage, I started to realize how unhappy I was. I felt like I had no identity of my own. One Saturday night, my husband was invited to a poker party at my parent's house, *guys only*, so my mom and I went out to a bar called Freddie's Tavern. First mistake we made was to start drinking and not eat dinner, and then we joined a booth of *lawyers* and started doing watermelon shots. I could really drink back then and at twenty-three I was some kind of *hot*.

We closed the bar and to this day, I don't know how I drove a car, but I got my mom home and the poker game was still going on. Without saying a word to any of the poker players, including my husband, I left and drove fifteen-miles to a friend's house. I had been there once before when he needed a ride home from work. As I pulled into his driveway, I remembered him saying he never locked his doors. He had a male roommate, and I guess lucky for me I chose my friend's bedroom, crawled-in next to him and ended my first marriage.

CHAPTER 40

TED

Ted high-tailed it out of the campground and many campers noticed the blood on the old man's shirt and how he was no longer using his cane. He bounded into his truck and raced out of the gas station entrance. Fags, it was all their fault. Instead of a stealth mission it was a major *snafu*. Even with his fake plates, he knew it would only be a matter of time before they identified his truck.

He took the next exit off the highway then drove at least five-miles before he spotted a dusty dirt side road. The smell of fag blood on his shirt and gloves made him nauseous. Ted finally came upon a driveway that snaked-back into a clearing. Perfect, there was a barn where he could stash his truck and a sweet shiny new red Ford F-250 pickup parked out front.

Ted hit the brakes, jumped out, and quickly went around to the bed of the truck to find a clean shirt in his duffel bag. He tossed his bloody shirt and gloves in the toolbox, took a deep breath, and then walked casually up to the front door. Ted knocked, then rang the doorbell and anxiously waited for someone to answer the door. The smell of coffee, fried potatoes, and what he hoped was sausage teased his senses; thankfully the food combo replaced the smell of that freak's blood. The door opened and much to his surprise an extremely short, older woman answered the door and asked, "What business do you have here?"

Caught off-guard by the woman, Ted said, "I'm lost and need directions."

The old woman said, "Leave my driveway and go back the way you came!"

Then she slammed the door in Ted's face and he heard the deadbolt click. Ted's stomach growled and he thought it was so rude of her to not give him directions or offer him something to eat. He was unsure if there was anyone else at home, seeing that some pint-sized woman would be too small to drive an F-250, but he took a chance. He went around to the back of the house, opened the screen door and kicked-in the six-pane wood door—which, if he would have tried the door knob, was unlocked. He saw there was only one place setting on the table and knew she was alone.

The startled old woman screamed at him and ran to the closet to get her gun. She opened the closet door and Ted pushed her inside and grabbed the gun as the woman fell to the floor. He closed the door, pushed the couch across the room to barricade her in the closet, and took the gun with him into the kitchen.

She was screaming and yelling, "Let me out you big rat!"

Ted yelled from the kitchen, "Mom, you're finally getting what you deserve; you locked the doors so I couldn't eat and now I've locked *you* away from the food so you can starve to death."

The woman stopped yelling and listened while the crazy stranger finished his rant. With her stomach growling, she heard him finish cooking breakfast and then sit down and eat it. When the old woman didn't think things could get worse, she heard the water running and that bastard was actually whistling while taking a shower in her bathtub. Scrubbing himself thoroughly in the shower, Ted looked for body wash hoping to find some that smelled like the kind the Missus or Frances used, but only found Dial soap—it would have to work to get the fag-smell off of him.

The old woman listened as he finished his shower, left the house and started his truck, but she heard him drive only so far. He returned to the house, rummaged through the cupboards, and then found the Ford truck keys hanging by the backdoor on the key rack her grandson had made for her years ago while he was in Cub Scouts.

The stranger tapped on the door and said, "The average human can live for seven-days without water and thirty-days without food, but you look pretty below-average to me and old, so I give you a few days before you die."

The old woman said nothing back to the beast, heard the front door open and then slam shut. The stranger roared-off in her new Ford F-250 truck.

"Bastard, I'll teach him," the old woman snarled. She then stepped to the side of the closet and opened the trap door that led to the crawl space below. She thought to herself, I'll show you *below-average* as she broke open the outside storm cellar door with a shovel and a good kick.

Fifteen-minutes later two Truckee police officers and the Nevada County Sheriff were on the scene and processing Ted's truck and other units were now in hot pursuit of a bright red Ford F-250. Ted should have never messed with the old woman's new truck.

Chapter 41

FRANCES

I switched the television off and sat there in the dark feeling first sorry for myself, then sorry for all the relationships I had destroyed; one right after another. Why did I always do that? My parents had been married for over twenty-five years before my dad died at the young age of forty-six, and the majority of my relatives were all happily married. Annie and her husband had just recently celebrated thirty-five years of wedded bliss, so what was wrong with me? My parent's marriage had been infused with physical and verbal fights, usually fueled by alcohol, but I never felt insecure about them breaking-up.

I was always the one to end the relationships. Every time I would find reasons to end it—even if I had to embellish, or as Martin would phrase it, make *counterfactual assertions*, about my partner's faults. Oh, the dirty little secrets I bore, and yet in explaining why I was leaving the relationship, the blame all fell on the guys. I rarely took any responsibility. When I was living back home with my parents during my first divorce, I followed my dad's advice.

He said, "If you're changing one part of your life, you should change all of it."

So I quit my high-paying job at Coors, moved into an eight-by-sixteen-foot trailer and worked for $1.35 an hour, plus tips, as a breakfast waitress in a small fishing town called Grand Lake. I had no benefits, except for a free meal each day and I usually took in about ten-dollars in tips daily.

After barely making a living in the remote fishing village, I headed for Castle Rock and enrolled in a barber college. I was single and starting my life over, *again*, and since my father had just recently passed-away I decided to move to the *Rock* to be closer to my sister and her husband and begin a new career, and a new life. One day, I was working on a customer while still in barber college, when a cocky hairstylist walked into the school. He had long hair, nice clothes and was a very talented stylist.

It didn't take long for the two of us to hook-up, but not in that way. He was very respectful and we seemed to have a good relationship. We dated on-and-off for a year, and then tied the knot. After getting married, I could probably count on one-hand the amount of times we had sex before I became pregnant. It was a miracle to me that Sophie was ever conceived. In retrospect, that was a very confusing time in my life and then after Sophie was born, my whole world revolved around her. Due to my pregnancy and not taking real good care of myself, I had lost my shape and my husband was revolted by my looks.

It would take me hours to do my hair, makeup and get dressed to go out and then he would ask me, "Are you really going out looking like that?"

We seemed more like roommates or quarreling siblings, than a married couple. He had remained a hairstylist while I left the barbershop to work at a real estate appraisal firm. Then, planning ahead for when Sophie was in school, I found a job in a school district so I would have summers off with my daughter. I worked the second-shift in the substitute teacher office from 1:00 to 9:00 PM scheduling substitutes for all the schools in the district. I also worked on Sunday nights from 6:00 to 10:00 PM scheduling subs for Mondays to make sure all the classes were covered.

Money was tight, so since my husband's hair salon was closed and I didn't report to work until 4:30 PM on Mondays; I cleaned the salon in order to make extra money—a whopping fifteen-dollars a day. One morning, after cleaning all the nasty hair and who knows what else from the floors and counters, I saw that one of the drawers had a lot of hair in it. I figured I should clean all the renegade hair out of the drawers so I got to work. Little did I realize what I was about to find. It seemed that the partners had much more in common that owning the salon. I found a series of love letters between the two that made me realize why there wasn't any sex going on at my house.

Shaking and sick to my stomach, I left the shop, went home, took a long hot shower, got dressed for work and when I got to my office I made copies of their correspondence. I felt like I'd been kicked in the gut and stabbed in the heart. I dropped the love letters back at the shop before I drove home and then crawled in bed next to Sophie.

The next night I invited Sophie's dad out to a local restaurant, and I confronted him about his indiscretion. You should have seen the stares from the tables all around us. That was October. In December, we took Sophie to Disneyland and Knott's Berry Farm for the holidays. We bought her the Barbie horse she wanted for Christmas, came home, sat her down and told her we were getting a divorce. In retrospect, I wonder how confusing it must have been for Sophie to go to the Magical Kingdom only to return home and have her life shattered. This was a lot for a five-year-old child to digest in such a short time. I swore it would be different if I ever married again.

CHAPTER 42

TED

The old woman's truck had all the bells and whistles! Ted hit the CD button and a Loretta Lynn song came on, sorry Loretta not today. He hit the radio and pushed *seek* to find a station. As bad as the morning began, things were now looking up. He had a full belly, took a nice hot shower and had a new red pickup truck. The radio interrupted his happy thoughts, "Next up, the latest song from Taylor Swift, but first we have breaking news to report . . ."

After the news flash, the truck seemed like it was spinning out of control. They were reporting on two deaths, and another man in critical condition at a Truckee campground, gave a description of a tall man with gray hair, ball cap and a white truck which had already been recovered in a local barn. Then the news got even worse, Ted heard the old woman's voice on the radio and her description of what happened at her house that morning and her missing truck, a new bright red Ford F-250. He could kick himself for not snapping her scrawny, wrinkled little neck when he had the chance.

Without even reaching an exit, Ted launched the truck off the highway and onto the frontage road. He took the next right and decided he would take back roads until he found another ride. First Fred, then only two dead at the campground and the old woman was alive—how had she escaped from the closet? Ted felt like he was losing his edge. Focus, Ted focus! He was still hours away from the next phase of his mission when he realized he could be stopped by police at any time driving this massive bright red truck. He immediately ditched the truck, grabbed his menial belongings, and started running as fast as he could to distance himself from the F-250.

He counted fifteen cars that passed his outstretched thumb. Then lucky number sixteen stopped and asked, "Where to?"

Ted said, "How about the coast?"

The young driver said, "I can take you as far as Sacramento."

"Beggars can't be choosers, Sacramento is fine with me!"

Feeling relieved, Ted got in the boy's rusty Chevy Blazer and they were off. The driver was a clean-shaven young man who was listening to a baseball game on the radio. The two guys talked about great players of the past and present, and then Ted dated himself when he talked about his all-time favorite player—Don Larsen. Ted told the driver that he was born on the day Don Larsen threw a perfect game for the Yankees in the 1956 World Series.

The driver said, "I've heard of Larsen and his perfect game, but I'm a huge Cardinals fan, and no one was more exciting to watch than Albert Pujols. I play first base for my high school team, just like Pujols. I can't believe they actually traded him!"

Ted liked this kid and told him, "I'm a die-hard Yankees fan and even named my dog, Yankee."

When the young man reached his destination, Ted gave him twenty-dollars for gas, and told him, "Today you are the luckiest kid in the world," and walked away.

As chance would have it, there was a bus station nearby and a bus headed to the coast in a little over an hour. Ted had time to grab a bite to eat, check the news, and be on his way to the *most beautiful place on Earth*, as his fiancée referred to it the first time they visited the campsite and surrounding areas. After he ate, Ted entered the air-conditioned bus, and settled down in a seat next to no one. He stretched out over both seats, dozed-off, and then started to dream about his last visit to Wildcat.

Breathtaking views, cliffs, sea caves, sea lions, waterfalls, the privacy, and yes, even the skunks. He remembered how they spit toothpaste around the perimeter of their tent to keep the pesky varmints away. The camp had one way in, a seven-mile dirt double-track trail that you had three means of traversing: by foot, mountain bike or by horse.

When the bus stopped at his destination, the city of Point Reyes Station by the coast, uncharacteristically Ted thanked the bus driver, gave him a five-dollar tip, and found that the streets were rolled-up at ten o'clock in this small town. He walked to the visitor's center and looked at the map stapled to the outside bulletin board. He needed to get to the Five Brooks

Trailhead. From town it would be an eight-mile hike, in the dark, and then another seven-mile trek on the trail to get to the Wildcat Camp. Ted decided to wait until morning, rent a bike and find out who will not be having a good day. He found a park bench and lay down for the night.

Chapter 43

FRANCES

Tossing and turning, I gave up on sleep and did another channel-check on the television. It was the middle of the night and I was not in the mood for infomercials or repeats of Two & a Half Men. I turned off the TV and I stared out each window and saw nothing of importance. I then curled up in a chair with a blanket. I returned to my earlier recollections and my last thought about how different it would be if I married again.

Well, after divorce number two, I met a man at the grocery store. He was a real estate agent that specialized in mountain properties. I found someone who was strong, serious, stable and available. I wanted my daughter to have a safe environment in which to live and my one-bedroom apartment across from a Kwik-way and on a busy street was not the answer. His house wasn't much better, but he also came with a twenty-acre wooded vacant lot in the foothills west of Castle Rock where he wanted to build his dream home.

Before we built *his* dream home, and while we were dating, the red-flag warnings began appearing. Why didn't I pay attention to them?

There was the time Sophie spilled her milk on his wood dining room table. He threw a major fit and screamed endlessly at Sophie—she was only six-years-old. He had brought the wooden table all the way back from the Naval Station in Rota, Spain, where he was stationed for five-years. I understood the sentimentality behind the wood table, but his reaction was just too bizarre aimed at a small child who accidentally spilled a glass of milk.

Then there were the weekend nights when Sophie was at her dad's house and we would sit at home in silence reading Time, Newsweek, or outdoor magazines—no music, no television, no conversation. The only break in the reading routine was at nine o'clock on Saturday night. The magazine he was reading was carefully placed back in the rack and he would say, "Let's go."

Dutifully I stood up, walked to the bedroom and had our weekly sex for approximately four-minutes. No kissing and no foreplay—just a man relieving himself. Although I knew this wasn't healthy for any relationship, I was almost thankful it was only once a week.

Remembering back even further, it had been a couple weeks after we began dating, that we went on a run in Castlewood Canyon. It was a challenging seven-mile run complete with scrambling down steep banks, crossing a small stream and the threat of rattlesnakes—he left me in his dust.

When I finally finished the course, I said, "Wow, I almost kept up with an ex-Marine."

He had been seated on a rock, but after my comment he jumped to his feet, stood erect and his six-foot three-inch frame looked like he was ten-feet tall, puffed out his chest, glared down at me, and bellowed, "There are only two *ex*-Marines, Lee Harvey Oswald and John Wayne Bobbitt."

I felt like the wind had been knocked out of me. I understood the Oswald inference, but why Bobbitt? He ran back to his truck and didn't speak to me the rest of the day. This was one of those major red-flag warnings and I missed it.

There were other situations, but now they all seem so trivial. On Saturday mornings, before going on trail runs, bike rides, or hikes, we would clean the house top to bottom with straight Pinesol. It would take at least two-days for that strong smell to dissipate and then we'd do it all over again. We lived together for ten-months before we got married and I never once was allowed to answer his house phone. Even though we were adults, he was afraid his parents would find out about Sophie and me living with him and not being married. I respected his wishes, but it still seemed a little weird to me.

I never realized what a loner he was until we planned our wedding and he only wanted close family. We had eleven guests total at the ceremony, store-bought cake and iced tea. The honeymoon, (yes, we did have sex on our honeymoon—it was a Saturday night after all), was a camping trip in the San Juan mountain range in southwestern Colorado. The day after our wedding we rode Lizard Head Pass, elevation 10,222 feet on our road bikes. It was the hardest thing I'd ever done. The ascent was painful, but the descent was petrifying. Once you are at the top of the pass you have tremendous views. But as a rider on extremely skinny little tires, navigating narrow switchbacks, it was terrifying to have about ten-inches of pavement on the shoulder while sharing the road with truckers and vacationers in their RV's and trailers. My fear of heights also left me paralyzed when I'd glance over the edge and see how far I could possibly fall.

My new husband's endearing words to me once I reached the summit were, "What took you so long?"

His dad absolutely loved Sophie, but his mother could never get over the fact that I was divorced and Sophie was not her son's *real* daughter. My father-in-law loved me, too. Whenever we would visit them I'd make him burritos and green chili. My mother-in-law would be furious because he loved my cooking. Her normal dinner was a head of iceberg lettuce cut in half, set on a plate, and an over-cooked frozen pizza.

One night, the pizza crust actually caught fire in the oven and she took it out, smacked the pizza on the counter to smother the flames, and then served it for dinner—burnt bottom crust and all! Breakfast was always a bowl of Corn Flakes, a banana, and weak-ass instant Sanka coffee. Lunch was always a Spam sandwich with mustard on white bread. The lack of food choices left us starving and me being a vegetarian, the food at my in-laws just didn't cut it. Sophie and I would sneak-off to a little Mexican market where no one spoke English, but we could gorge ourselves on some good food.

Sophie and I managed to work within the strict routine and decided that living in this beautiful house in the lush foothills of Castle Rock was, in her words, "Not *that* bad."

Still there were some strange times. After dinner, we were washing the dishes. I handed Sophie the green ceramic bowl, he had to be served his salad in every night, and it slipped from her hands, hit the tile floor and shattered. I swept up the pieces, put them in the trash, and then the rapture began. I told him what happened, that I dropped the bowl and it broke. He began going through the trash picking out every single piece of the bowl except for one piece that must have slid under the refrigerator. He then painstakingly glued each piece back together. He did not speak to either of us for two-weeks, but every night I made his salad precisely the way he wanted it. Lettuce in bite-sized pieces, baby spinach, chopped fresh broccoli, grated carrot, sprinkled with oat bran, wheat bran and wheat germ, with one-tablespoon of dressing, and always in his glued-together green ceramic bowl. The bowl was missing one piece that I had recovered from under the fridge and spitefully taken to work with me and thrown away.

It was during this time, that I had returned to college to obtain my teaching license and started teaching high school English. I relished the escape from the daily routine at home and loved every minute of being a teacher. I'd get up early before he did just so I wouldn't have to see him in the mornings. Sophie would get herself to school, even though she was just in third grade, the bus stop for the elementary school she attended was right at the end of our driveway.

Living with my husband was more mental anguish than any physical abuse. His stare could melt an iceberg. The only time I remember him physically touching Sophie was when she was sitting at the breakfast counter eating; we never used his wood table anymore. He came up behind her and put his thumb under her collarbone and told her that that was how he was trained to subdue the enemy. Sophie said nothing, my feet were frozen to the floor across the kitchen, and then he left the room. I ran to Sophie and swore he'd never touch her again.

Valentine's Day was approaching and I handmade a card for Sophie and the last line said, "Remember, YOU are the most important person in this whole wide world to me, I love you more than anyone. Love, Mom." It would be amazing to me how explosive a few loving words from a mom to a daughter could be.

My husband received a call from his mother to inform us that his father had a brain tumor and didn't have much time left. Les was never one to complain or go to the doctor, so his tumor had gone undetected for years. We found out the news right after our major blow-up over Sophie's Valentine's Day card, so things were a bit tense between us. We flew out to the coast and were *greeted* by his mother. After she almost got us killed pulling out of the airport parking lot, as usual she crossed herself before merging onto the highway, and we silently rode back to their house.

Les looked frail, but his eyes lit-up when he saw Sophie and me. We hugged, cried, laughed, and then told stories all while my husband and his mother stared at the three of us, but never spoke a word. He asked me if I would make him burritos and green chili and of course I did—much to my mother-in-law's chagrin. She refused to eat what I cooked and said that my cooking would kill him. Les just rolled his eyes, winked at Sophie, and ate another burrito.

I was glad for our quality time with Les, but it was when we were leaving that sealed the deal on me leaving marriage number three. It was how my husband said goodbye to his dying dad. We knew Les only had a short time to live and my husband shook his father's hand and said, "Goodbye."

He then turned rigidly and walked out of the room. No hug, no take care, and no I love you, nothing. I can still picture the pain in his Les's eyes as he had sadly accepted his son's hand and said, "Goodbye, Ted."

Chapter 44

WILDCAT CAMP

Doing something forbidden is always more fun than following the rules. Ruby waited outside her best friend's house for Lon to come pick her up. Ruby's girlfriend said she would cover for her in case her mom called. Lon's parents thought he was at an overnight camping trip with his three best buddies. Lon didn't have any buddies, but his parents were none the wiser. His imaginary buddies were Nick, Joe, and Kevin, all names he borrowed from the Jonas Brothers. He used these names when calling Ruby so his parents didn't know he was meeting or even talking to her on his cell phone.

His parents had restricted him from seeing Ruby because she was not Asian and her father was a minister at the local Baptist church. Ruby's parents had also forbidden Ruby from seeing Lon because of his race and religion. Ruby and Lon often spoke of how much they were like Romeo and Juliet. Ruby just turned sixteen and Lon was almost eighteen, and they knew their parents were wrong to judge people by their ethnicity and religious beliefs. They also knew a love like theirs would last forever.

Lon parked his car at the curb and said, "Hey beautiful, need a ride?"

Ruby tossed her bag into the back seat then slid into his car and said, "Yes, Romeo I do!"

She ducked-down in the front seat and put her head on his lap so if anyone would see Lon driving through town they would not see her. Plus, she liked the excitement she felt by having her head on his thigh. They had never done more than kiss, well maybe a little fondling, but tonight they were going to go all the way.

Ruby giggled and told Lon, "I brought a slinky black negligee that I *borrowed* from my older sister's panty drawer."

Excitedly Lon said, "Well I brought some wine in a mayonnaise jar that I siphoned-off from my parent's stock a little at a time so they wouldn't notice."

Teasingly Ruby said, "I'm too young to drink—take me home!"

Playfully she squeezed his thigh and Lon thought to himself that if Ruby kept touching him, he would explode. He tried to get his mind off of her hand and told Ruby, "I also brought candles—unless you are too young for them and my I-pod with your favorite songs to set the mood."

"To set the mood for what, might I ask?" They both laughed and Ruby finally sat up and rested her head on Lon's shoulder.

Lon and Ruby were both nervous as they reached Point Reyes Station, rented bikes, and then drove to their destination. At the Five Brooks Trailhead they packed what they needed for the night and began their seven-mile trek on the Stewart Trail to a place they heard of that was isolated and had a beautiful view from atop the cliffs where they would set up camp. Lon liked the place already just because of the campground's name, Wildcat.

CHAPTER 45

TED

Ted had slept so soundly he did not hear the approaching footsteps. A thump on his foot startled him upright. Only a few feet from his face stood a policeman in full uniform. The officer held a nightstick in his left hand while resting his right hand on his revolver.

"No loitering, now move along," that was all the officer said and he was gone.

After Ted's heart returned to normal, he felt a renewed sense of hope and invincibility that this would indeed be his lucky day—Phase Seven was about to commence.

He waited outside the Black Mountain Cycles bike shop until it opened at 7:30 AM, rented a bike and was on the road by 7:45 AM. After a great night sleep, he was sharp and focused on the task at hand. He had eight-miles on pavement and seven-miles of double-track mountain bike trail to reach his destination, Wildcat Camp. He checked the log-in sheet at the trailhead to make sure there were campers and much to his delight there were seven names written in the register.

Ted was sure the scenery was beautiful that surrounded him, but all he was focused on was the trail ahead. Reaching Wildcat he felt the coolness of the Pacific and heard the waves crashing against the shore below. As he rode closer to the cliffs, he could see tents, but no people.

There was a light fog above the area and he peered over the cliff to see if the campers were on the beach below. Two people were down to the south of his vantage point washing off in the cascading waterfall. One man was jogging away from the campsites down the steep trail that was the only route to the beach. Another couple could be seen by the sea caves to the north taking pictures of sea lions bobbing-up and down in the surf. That left two campers unaccounted for.

He listened outside of each tent and heard some movement in the fourth tent. He could barely hear the voices, but was ecstatic to recognize a male and female voice. He did not want a reoccurrence of what happened in Truckee. Ted's ex-wife always called him homophobic and if there was a word for it she was the exact opposite. She had relatives, both male and female, in San Francisco that were repulsively in same sex marriages and even had kids.

Shaking his head he came back to the present and removed one of his trusty zip ties from his pocket and quietly secured the tent's door zipper so it could not be opened. He then went over to the bikes, which there were only six—one person must have hiked back on foot, and then Ted slashed all twelve tires and even the spare inner tubes.

Ted went back to the occupied tent, pulled the stakes out, and started to drag the tent and the horrified campers to the edge of the cliff.

The young man began screaming, "Hey, what are you doing? This is not funny! Are you crazy? Let go of the damn zipper! C'mon man!"

Pleading with the stranger, the young girl begged him, "Please leave us alone. Please stop it! Lon do something!"

Just then, Ted started to lose his footing near the edge of the fifty-foot drop and grabbed onto the tent. He felt a foot kicking at him and the side window unzipped and he saw his next terrified victims—a young, naked Asian male and a homely red-headed freckled-face girl probably no older than fifteen in black lace.

They shrieked at him and tore at the window screen. Ted regained his footing, got behind the tent and sent it sailing over the cliff. Screams could barely be heard over the crashing surf and Ted was on his bike before the tent hit the beach. That was too much like work, Ted thought, whistling on his way back down the trail enjoying the scenery.

CHAPTER 46

FRANCES

When Martin arrived in Coronado, he had the taxi driver let him off two-blocks from the Coronado Inn, and I spotted him the minute he exited the cab. He was in his typical flannel-plaid shirt, Wranglers and a camo hat—a bit out of place in Coronado, but what a welcomed sight. I watched Martin with one bag slung over his shoulder try to jog down the sidewalk in his cowboy boots.

I could tell by the look on his face that he was worried when he saw the police cars in the parking lot of the Inn. He ran across Orange Avenue against traffic with horns blaring and drivers swearing at him. Martin reached for my door and was greeted by a burly police officer.

"Officer, that is my husband, please let him in." I said choking back my tears.

I fell into Martin's outstretched arms and sobbed, I was so glad to see him. After a quick squeeze, I breathed in Martin's essence and told him of the recent developments.

"Martin, I called the police after I saw the news this morning. Two men were murdered and one critically injured in a campground up in Truckee. The description given by the bystanders at the campground of the man seen fleeing in a white truck was the same man I saw last night leaving the parking garage."

Without any warning, Martin punched the wall behind me and yelled, "I hate you, Ted!"

After regaining his composure, and after apologizing to all of us, Martin began sharing the items he brought from home with the police. The day he had talked to me about my junior high yearbook and note from an old boyfriend, he also found an envelope with a Far Side cartoon about vegetarians, a campsite receipt from Portola Redwoods State Park, and a letter from Ted that begged me to come home and the letter ended with, *you can take this to your grave, no one will ever love you as much as I do.* The envelope was postmarked with the month and year that our divorce was final.

Had he been planning this deadly rampage all these years? It didn't make sense; he had remarried only a few months after our divorce. Martin also informed the police about Ted's *supposed* death and how the body was never officially identified, but he had been declared legally dead. Was that the beginning, over a year ago of these tragic deaths? I had been working with the police on a timeline in regard to the newspapers, the common articles about young couples and the locations, and now I added another dead body to the list—the one we thought was Ted.

Just then, Martin took out the campsite receipt and asked, "Officers, do you know the number of the campsite where the first murdered couple was found?"

The officer responded, "A-14, why?"

Martin handed the officer the campsite receipt he held in his hand. It read: Portola Redwoods State Park, Campsite A-14, July 27, 1993.

I thought back to that campsite in the redwoods and fell on the bed. That was where Ted had proposed to me so many years ago. It was all coming back to me. We drove all day and night to get to a redwood forest; we only stopped to buy a case of peaches in Palisade, Colorado, for gas, to pee, and at the border where I was so afraid we'd be busted for sneaking fruit into California.

Ted proposed to me that night under a full moon—although it seemed more like an edict. The next day we spent riding our bikes in the redwoods, and then headed for the coast. I had a poster I framed from Point Reyes in my bedroom at home in Colorado, but took it down because there was a sea lion with bulging eyes that gave Martin the creeps.

We then went to Petaluma to ride Cattlemen's Trail. I hated that trail because of all the hills and we got caught in a terrible rain and lightning storm. We attended a ballgame in Oakland and I remembered that Dennis Eckersley was the closer. On our trip home, we stayed in Truckee—I remembered I had nightmares because of the gruesome stories Ted told me about the Donner Party. We had sailed in San Diego Bay with his dad, but that was when we visited his parents on a separate trip from our vacation up north. Another place we visited though was a campground on top of some cliffs, but I was struggling to remember the name.

Martin said, "Wildcat."

I looked at him in disbelief, "How did you know?"

"Frances, I think the sea air has washed away some brain cells. Don't you remember when we wrote out our wills a few years ago, you said you wanted your ashes spread from the top of these amazing cliffs at the most beautiful place on Earth, Wildcat."

The air went out of the room—that was where he would strike next. He committed some murders out of sequence, like the deaths at the Oakland A's game and Navy Yacht Club, but they were all places the two of us had visited. Why hadn't I been able to make the connections sooner? The police confirmed that this was more than a coincidence. They radioed the police in Point Reyes Station and the Marin County Sheriff, and then the officer in charge requested they send reinforcements to the Wildcat campground and surrounding areas. They also sent a unit to the villa to search my apartment, and the parking garage across the street since that was where I saw Ted exiting in his white truck. Martin held on to me as the enormity of the situation hit both of us like a ton of bricks.

CHAPTER 47

TED

The ride back to the trailhead was much easier because he had to climb to get to the Wildcat campground, so now it was a downhill cruise. Ted encountered a group of five bikers loaded down with camping gear headed toward the campsites.

He had nothing to hide from these people, so he waved and said, "What a beautiful morning, you should all feel lucky you're alive, enjoy your stay."

He smiled at the teenage girl whose budding breasts smiled back at him trying to escape her pink biking shirt. The girl did not meet his leering gaze, but focused on the man's tattoo. It was a black and gold cobra with fangs jutting-out and the body snaking all the way down his left arm with its tail ending on the back of his hand.

Passing the last mile-marker for the trail, Ted could faintly hear police sirens. Not taking any chances, he left the trail and detoured into the rough terrain. The only thing he could fathom was that one of the campers had a SAT phone, or that someone in town recognized him from the Truckee reports. Staying about fifty-yards off the trail, but continuing toward the main road, Ted heard the sirens getting louder and the sound of ATVs racing-up the mountain bike trail.

His covert training would pay off as he ditched his bike under some fallen timbers and went the remainder of the way on foot. He skirted the trailhead which had police cars from Point Reyes and sheriff cars from Marin County blocking the exit. Even though he wore long biking pants, Ted's legs were bleeding from the rugged terrain. Finally, he reached the main road about a mile from the trailhead. He saw a gas station down the road and stayed hidden in the trees until he felt it was safe to cross the street without being detected.

Ted watched as a young twenty-something woman filled her car up with gas and then went inside to pay. He opened her back car door and folded his large frame onto the floor. He found a suitcase, towel and some dirty clothes to cover him and waited for his chauffeur to return. A few minutes went by and he almost hopped-in the front seat and drove the car himself—people always leave their keys in the ignition when they get gas, but he knew the police would be in hot pursuit of a stolen vehicle. Shifting his weight he could hear footsteps, lucky he was lying with his deaf ear down, and then the car door opened, she put food down on the seat so close to his nose he could almost taste it, and placed her drink in the cup holder.

His stomach growled at the same moment she started her car and they flew out of the gas station. He knew they were headed south because she didn't turn and her car had been pointed in that direction. Her music blaring, she ate chips and a hot dog, and then turned her CD off and answered her vibrating cell phone.

"Hey, no way, okay, I will be careful, no hitchhikers see you soon. I'm just leaving PR Station and should be in LA around five or so, love ya too."

Could that have been someone warning her about a killer on the loose? Am I that famous that she's driving me to Hollywood? Ted tried to relax and focus on the final phase of his mission. Barring any major delays, flat tires, long rest stops, he should be back in Coronado by eight or nine. He wondered if he asked the woman to drive faster, if it would freak her out. Ted figured he had better just lay low until her next stop and get as far out of Dodge as he could. See you soon, Sophie.

CHAPTER 48

FRANCES

The report from Wildcat was not good. Two teenagers had been killed when their tent, with them inside, was thrown off a cliff at the edge of the campground. To add to the horrific news, a family of five identified a rider that fit Ted's description and said he was headed back to the trailhead. Officers drove up the trail and all the way to the campsite, but did not see any sign of him. The time frame and location where the family had seen Ted would have been close to when the officers arrived and the sirens must have alerted him.

Roadblocks were in place at either end of the highway outside the city and the officers were optimistic that he couldn't get too far. They were also broadcasting a news alert on the radio to warn all travelers in the area to be on the lookout for anyone fitting Ted's description and that he was extremely dangerous.

After the briefing, I wanted to return to the villa and check on my cats, the Missus, Rosie and Juanita. When Martin and I arrived back at the compound, we found the police searching the grounds, the villa, and the apartment. The Missus, still in her dressing-gown ordered the police to take their shoes off before entering the house. Mister L left and said he had a tee-time. Rosie and Juanita were huddled together by the side of the garage. Rosie had identified Ted as the sailor who had met her at the gate and handed her the newspaper that he said I had dropped.

Police also located Ted's base of operation in the parking garage across the street and asked Martin and me to join them. They explained that a janitor had been killed in this room months ago, the case had never been solved, and the room had been sealed. A condominium resident identified Ted's white truck and one remembered the DOD plates, but not the actual numbers. I was sickened when we entered the small room with the surveillance equipment, map of California with numbers handwritten on it, sleeping bag, hot plate and mini-fridge.

I sat on the lone folding chair then jumped up immediately because I realized Ted had sat on this chair and watched my movements and listened to all my conversations—even chats I had with myself. I went over to the clothes hanging on the pipe and fixated on the Navy uniform. His dad had served in the Navy so proudly for over forty-years; from battles in the Pacific during World War II, to fighting in Korea, and even a tour off the shores of Vietnam.

The last time I saw our son Nick, was when he was wearing this same Navy uniform before he was deployed to the Persian Gulf. Martin had spoken to him a few times in the past month, but communication was highly restricted from Nick's location. The last time I heard from Nick was a brief phone call on Mother's Day, but not a word from him a month later on my birthday. I sent him letters, well actually picture postcards from Coronado and San Diego at least once a week. He had been stationed here in Coronado for three-years prior to his deployment and when he talked to Martin he always said how much he missed the island.

Martin's hand on my shoulder made me flinch, but what he pointed to made me scream. Next to the map was a picture of Sophie when she was about ten. She was sitting on the deck at our *dream* home and her fingers were making the sign-language symbol for, *I love you.* Her adorable picture was thumb-tacked to a Valentine's Day card. I explained to the officers who was in the photo and asked if I could see the card. A picture of our dog, Yankee, *Kee-kee* for short, with a red bow around her neck and the words, *be mine*, written in a bubble next to her mouth.

I opened the card and tears poured down my face. Where I had originally printed, *Dear Sophie*, Sophie's name was scratched-out and *Ted*, was written in its place.

This was the card I made years ago for Sophie that angered Ted so much. It said, *Happy Valentine's Day. I just wanted you to know how proud of you I am. Remember, YOU are the most important person in this whole wide world to me, I love you more than anyone. Love, Mom.*

Before I could reach for my phone, Martin had already dialed Sophie's number. No answer, so he left a voicemail. Next, he tried her husband's cell, no answer, and then he remembered it was the start of archery season and Harlan and his son Brett were gone hunting. I tried our daughter's phone again and my call also went to voicemail. Sophie and her family had just moved to a new town and I didn't know anyone in that town to call.

"Officer, can you please contact the Alamosa Police Department to do a welfare check on my daughter . . ."

CHAPTER 49

TED

Women drivers! Did she have to hit every pothole in the road? Ted was starving, had to pee and his legs kept cramping. She also listened to one bad CD after another. He knew at the next pit-stop he was getting out and taking care of business. Forty-five minutes later, but what seemed like an eternity, he felt the car slow down, heard the turn signals clicking, and thankfully felt the car come to a stop. Ted waited for the female driver to exit the car and listened to hear if she was filling the car up with gas. No sound of the gas cap being removed or a nozzle being lifted, so he slowly sat up, tossed the suitcase, smelly clothes, and the towel off of him and took a quick look around.

He slowly opened the back car door, eased himself out and duck-walked over to the side of the car by the gas pump and tightened the gas cap so hard that only a brute could remove it. He stood erect and felt like his legs were protesting from inactivity and they would not move. Finally, one slow step after another, he entered the convenience store, headed straight for the men's room and passed his driver coming up the same aisle. Her arms were filled with chips, cookies, a bottled tea and a Snickers candy bar.

Exiting the head, Ted watched as his chauffeur waited in line to pay. He made his way to the front counter and stood behind his driver as she paid for her food purchases and pre-paid for her gas. Ted had grabbed a bag of Oreos, sunflower seeds, a bottle of water and a Snickers candy bar.

As he put his items down on the counter after his driver had paid, he sweetly yelled to her, "Oh miss, did you forget your candy bar?"

Ted held up the Snickers and she smiled, not even checking her bag, she came back, said thanks and returned to her car. He paid for his items, smiled at the clerk, and then left the store.

He started walking as if to leave the station and cross the street to an auto repair shop, when he heard a young female voice, "Excuse me sir, can you help me get my gas cap off? It seems to be stuck."

Ted smiled broadly as he approached the young woman and said, "Sometimes the gas tank creates a vacuum and will tighten the cap."

He grunted as he removed the gas cap and lifted the nozzle off the gas pump and started filling her tank. Who said chivalry was dead? His driver didn't protest, she told him, "You remind me of my grandpa, except my granddad is completely gray. He was in the military and also has tattoos, but his are faded and wrinkled."

Ted hoped she didn't see the veins pop-out in his neck and his nostrils flare as he kept pumping the gas. Ted was so vain he hated being likened to a *grandpa*.

"So, where are you headed?" he asked.

"Going to LA to hang with some friends," she responded while leaning against her car, "and you?"

"Well, I had been headed to Coronado to visit my daughter, but I'm stuck here until my car gets repaired." Ted nodded across the street to the closed repair shop. "The boys said it could take up to a week to fix and they're closed today so I can't even get my suitcase out of the trunk. I wanted to surprise her tonight for her birthday."

The tank was full and Ted removed the nozzle. The female driver then said, "How about a ride as far as LA? I can't leave you stranded here for your daughter's birthday."

"Are you sure? I don't want to impose on you."

"Don't give it another thought. I believe in karma and if I do something nice for someone, hopefully someone will do something nice for my granddad."

Putting his vanity aside, Ted said, "Thank you miss." He thought to himself, not all the story I told her was a lie. I am going to Coronado to surprise my daughter, step-daughter. With that thought he entered the car via the front passenger side and popped an Oreo in his mouth.

CHAPTER 50

SOPHIE

As Alamosa police officers knocked on her door, Sophie sat back in her airplane seat and closed her eyes. She was exhausted from their recent move and being left alone to unpack boxes while her husband and son went hunting. Dropping her daughter, Taylor, off at her granddad's house for the weekend, Sophie was excited to go to Coronado for a surprise visit to see her mom. It was so nice of Martin to pay for her airline ticket to San Diego, but he gave strict instructions not to talk to her mom and ruin the surprise. The other strange thing about this surprise visit was that Martin had only provided her with a one-way ticket.

Sophie got her carry-on bag from the overhead bin and thought to herself that if Harlan had been with her he would have retrieved her bag, and everyone else's bag because he was such an old-school kind of guy. Sophie smiled as she thought about her mom and how she raised her to be an independent woman—happy to be able to take care of herself, but she always appreciated a man with manners. She looked at the guy behind her and mentally labeled him a metro-sexual and figured he might break a nail if he got her bag down.

Exiting the plane, Sophie found her way outside to the taxi waiting-line and was glad to see there were only four people ahead of her in line. The smell of exhaust fumes and salt water engulfed her as she waited for a taxi.

The instructions Martin emailed to her said, *Take a taxi to the Fifth Avenue Ferry Landing, purchase a ticket for $3.50 cash only, and take the ferry to Coronado Island, then the metro nine-blocks to the Hotel Del Coronado. Check-in under my name, you'll have a spa treatment at two in the afternoon at the Spa at The Del, after that you have dinner reservations at 1500 Ocean at eight, then take a stroll out on the beach to the rock jetty, located northwest of the hotel, where your mom goes every night when it gets dark. Do not call* *your mom or answer her calls, remember this is a surprise! Have fun, don't worry about the cost, this special day is on me and will be worth every penny. I'll be at the cabin so I can't be reached. You can thank me when I see you again.*

The anticipation of surprising her mom gave Sophie butterflies in her stomach, but not being able to call her was killing her. They talked every day, but Sophie hadn't spoken to her in a couple days because she knew she wouldn't be able to keep this a secret. She remembered when her mom was staying at the cabin for ten straight days by herself so she could write her first book. After a few days without talking to her mom, Sophie got in her car and drove to the cabin to see if she was okay. They had never gone that long without talking.

It was going to be so good to see her mom again tonight. She knew from talking to her mom in past conversations that she liked to watch the sun set and enjoyed the tranquility of the beach when she almost had it all to herself. Her mom especially took pleasure on the beach by the rock jetty because of the sound the waves made when hitting the rocks. She always said that it was so rejuvenating like the ocean was cleansing her soul with the pounding and then peacefully retreating to the sea.

Sophie couldn't believe her luck—a free ticket to San Diego, staying at the Hotel Del Coronado, a relaxing spa treatment, dinner in a fancy restaurant, and a chance to finally see her mom after all these months. She wanted so badly to call her mom and have her join her at the spa, but just at that moment she felt the strong hands around her neck and her body went numb.

CHAPTER 51

FRANCES

Sophie's voicemail box was full and the Alamosa police said no one answered the door at Sophie's residence. The campus police received the authority to enter Sophie's apartment and see if anyone was inside. Martin and I held our breath until we heard that no one was found within the dwelling.

The officers did report though, that upon entering the kitchen they saw a note on the refrigerator that said, *Harlan and Brett, Left today (Saturday), Martin got me a ticket to San Diego to surprise my mom. Taylor is staying with my dad. It was a one-way ticket so I don't know when I'll be back. Hope hunting was good. Call me, love Sophie/Mom.*

There was dead silence in the room. The detective turned the speaker phone off and continued speaking privately to the Alamosa police giving them strict instructions to keep a surveillance team on the residence, but knew Ted would not show up there. Martin could only shake his head when the officer asked if he bought an airline ticket for Sophie. The question was answered as to Sophie's whereabouts, probably over the Rockies by now, and they also had a good hunch where Ted was headed.

I felt numb as I listened to the detective contact TSA officials and apprise them of the situation. With TSA help at the Pueblo, Denver, and San Diego airports, we learned that Sophie was on Frontier Flight 517 out of Denver, after being on a connecting flight from the small Pueblo airport, and that the flight had landed fifteen-minutes ago at the San Diego International Airport/Lindbergh Field. If Sophie had checked a bag she may still be in the airport, but the airlines said no checked baggage had been pre-paid for in her name.

The detective asked the airline officials to alert all security at the airport to be on the lookout for Sophie or Ted and sent pictures of both to identify either one. He gave one set of instructions if they located Sophie and more detailed instructions if they found Ted—with the caveat that he was definitely armed and extremely dangerous.

Sophie must be headed for Coronado. The police set up roadblocks on the west end of the Coronado Bay Bridge and began checking each vehicle exiting the bridge, or coming up the strand from Imperial Beach. What if Ted was at the airport and kidnapped her? My mind was swirling. Sophie was so close, but where was Ted?

Chapter 52

TED

A couple hours outside of Los Angeles, the odd couple, made a pit-stop and this time Ted paid for the gas, a carwash, and deli-sandwiches.

Ted was quite charming and even offered to drive. "Hey, I can drive for a while if you want to rest before you meet up with your friends."

"You know, I am a little tired of driving. Okay, but look for the Santa Monica sign, that's where we need to exit."

It didn't take long before he heard his driver softly snoring. Ted managed to drive the speed limit, even though he had to endure listening to a *Pink* CD over and over again. He was afraid to change to the radio in case there were reports about his whereabouts or description that might alert his passenger. After awhile, he started passing exit signs to Los Angeles.

About twenty-five miles south of the Santa Monica exit; the young lady stirred and asked, "Where are we?"

The sun was noticeably lower in the west and she could tell it was getting late. Ted was back in his mission mode and didn't respond. She saw a sign for Long Beach and knew they had missed her exit. She grabbed his arm and said, "Turn around, you missed my exit!"

Uncharacteristically, Ted smiled, apologized and exited the highway. He said, "Maybe you should drive since I am so unfamiliar with this part of California."

Ted told another small lie, but he was getting good at lying. As the young woman exited the car he sped off; leaving her in a cloud of dust. She ran a few steps, flipped him off and screamed, "Stop! You freakin' jackass! Bring my car back!"

Steaming mad she reached in her pocket for her cell phone to call 911 and realized her phone was gone. Her mom was going to kill her for losing her car and cell phone. What she thought was the unluckiest day of her life turned out to be her luckiest day ever.

Ted saw his enraged traveling companion in the rearview mirror and knew even if someone stopped to help her, he would still have time to make it to Coronado before being apprehended. While she *freshened-up* at their last stop he switched license plates with a car from Florida, the Sunshine State. With each mile he became more excited while he mentally prepared himself for the final phase of his mission. He wasn't sure who would be more surprised, Sophie or Frances.

The drive down Highway 5 was stop-and-go as usual, but he wasn't about to take his chances in the HOV lane to save some time. Ted was now in San Diego County and soon would be back in Coronado. Turning off his driver's annoying CD player he found a local radio station. Ted was famous! They knew his name, although the description made him sound like some wild beast or zombie returning from the dead. There was a warning to be on the look-out and to be careful because he was armed and dangerous. Armed? Ah yes, his hands are lethal weapons now aren't they?

As Ted approached the Coronado Bay Bridge, he turned the radio off and began to focus. He noticed cars backed-up for blocks prior to the on-ramp for the bridge. Was there an accident, roadblock or maybe a jumper? Locals got used to the bridge being closed due to people trying to commit suicide by jumping off the top of the bridge to their death in San Diego Bay below. Ted remembered an article he read that said the Coronado Bay Bridge ranked third in the U.S. for suicides and that there had been over two-hundred successful suicides since the bridge was opened in 1972. So, if the authorities were dealing with a jumper, then this was no big surprise.

He thought of driving down to Imperial Beach and up the strand, but knew if they were checking cars on the bridge and it wasn't closed for a jumper, then they'd be stopping cars on the strand entering Coronado. He decided to drive down by the Convention Center and ditch the car. Ted then popped into a corner store to take a leak, came out wearing a Padres baseball cap, and whistled while he walked a block down to the pier.

Leaning against a post, a young man in a white shirt and white shorts wearing a phony sailor hat asked, "Hey buddy, do you need a ride?"

Ted went to the ticket machine, purchased a water taxi ticket and never spoke a word to the young man, but for some reason made the driver very uneasy. Ted handed him his ticket and took a seat in the back of the water taxi. The driver didn't think twice about the man in the Padres hat, except for his piercing black eyes and that creepy tattoo. Most Padres fans, like his passenger, were walking around in a foul mood these days after the Giants beat them out for first place in the Western Division.

It only took eight-minutes for the water taxi to reach Coronado Island and the Ferry Landing. Not knowing if he out-smarted the police by not using the bridge or the strand, thirty-yards from the landing Ted slipped over the side of the taxi and swam to shore. It was dusk and no one noticed him.

The young man docked his taxi and turned to open the gate to allow his passenger off; except his passenger was gone. The driver looked on the dock to see if he had jumped onto the pier, but no one was in sight. He did see two police officers by the exit ramp, but decided against telling them about the rude Padres fan with the wicked tattoos. It was the end of his shift, he was tired, and he had a date. The man had left his baseball cap on the seat so the taxi-driver picked it up. He locked his taxi and then threw the hat in the trash can. The young man was originally from LA, was a die-hard Dodger's fan and hated the Padres.

CHAPTER 53

FRANCES

I paced back and forth at the make-shift command center just six-blocks north of the Hotel Del. The CBI, California Bureau of Investigation, had been apprised of the complex situation, but had not yet sent any support. It was late afternoon and no trace of Sophie. Every vehicle had been stopped that exited the bridge or was driven up the strand—all being searched for Sophie or Ted, but so far to no avail. Approximately forty-five minutes after Sophie's plane landed, the Coronado Police also posted two officers at the pier in case Sophie or Ted arrived in Coronado on the ferry or via a water taxi.

A report came in from the California State Patrol that said a female driver had her vehicle car-jacked on exit 85-A, and that she positively identified the picture officers showed her of Ted. She said he told her he was going to Coronado to surprise his daughter tonight for her birthday. The young woman then fainted when the police officer told her why Ted was on the run.

The car-jacked vehicle had been located by the Convention Center because it had been parked in a tow-away zone. They ran the Florida plates and the numbers did not match the vehicle identification number of the car. Officers tried the doors, which were left unlocked, and were able to get the correct information off the registration linking the car to the car-jacking. So now they knew he was close. He wouldn't make it over the bridge or up the strand, so where was he? The officers at the pier said they checked every passenger that left the ferry and all the water taxis were docked for the day, but no sign of Ted.

The police alerted all hotels and motels for Sophie's name and description, but no one reported seeing anyone matching her information. The largest hotel on the island, Hotel Del Coronado, said no one by that name had registered and numerous beautiful young ladies checked-in to their hotel daily—it would be impossible to remember every face. The police also solicited the hotels/motels for anyone matching Ted's description that possibly could be traveling with Sophie. Martin and I racked our brains for leads. Sophie knew my address at the villa so she could have possibly gone to the apartment, but the police had a team stationed there and had not seen either Sophie or Ted.

The Missus and her husband were ordered to stay inside their home with two (shoeless) police officers and go about their normal business in case Ted was watching them, too. Rosie and Juanita were also in the house and thrilled at the police presence and someone to actually talk to. There was also one female police officer in my apartment, who could pass for me from afar if Ted came back to observe my place from out on the street. The police did not think he would return to his room in the parking garage, but they left everything untouched in case he did come back. This is the scenario that they all wanted. For him to return to his hideout, the police seal the door and then trap him inside like a wild animal.

No sign of Sophie or Ted, and no phone calls—it was just an agonizing waiting game. The officers had been working the phones and walking the streets checking every store, restaurant, bar, beauty shop, boutique, any place a twenty-something female might go and they came up empty. Then, at about eight-fifteen that night, a phone call came in from Alamosa that would finally give us a break in the case.

CHAPTER 54

TED

Soaking wet, Ted did a belly crawl up the shoreline far enough from the Ferry Landing to not be seen and then continued to crawl to the back of a dumpster outside a condominium complex for some cover. Ted took off his shirt and wrung it out. Then he kicked his shoes off and removed his wet socks. He had to peel his pants off his wet skin and pulled his knife from its sheath on his ankle. He laid his pants on the asphalt and with one quick movement cut the legs off his biking pants, and made himself a pair of shorts. Ted put the wet shorts on, removed the sheath from his ankle, reinserted the razor-sharp knife and hid it in his pocket. Wet tennis shoes were not conducive to sneaking up on someone so he tossed them in the dumpster, put his cold clingy shirt back on, and started to walk barefoot back to the parking garage.

Ted kept to the alleyways and darted behind bushes if he saw any on-coming cars. It was getting close to oh-dark thirty and he needed to get to the beach in time for the final phase of his mission. He was nearing Seventh Street and Orange Avenue when he hid behind a church van to spy on the police building. As he watched the vanilla brick building with its ornate wrought iron fencing he had expected to see a flurry of activity, but surprisingly all he saw was Martin, of all people, outside talking on his cell phone. What the hell was Marty doing in Coronado? Ted wished he could hear who the asshole was talking to. Had that jerk flown out here to see Frances? Did he fly out with Sophie? Is the surprise on the beach for Frances ruined?

Just then, Frances appeared and he watched the estranged couple start walking down Orange Avenue possibly heading back to her apartment. He knew it was time to make his move; maybe they had finally connected the dots since his face was all over the news, but it was improbable that they found his hideout. How would they have figured that one out? Even if they had found his secret room, nothing in there could have given his plans away for tonight's surprise.

Ted had to think, should he abort the last phase of his mission or should he go ahead as planned? He decided not to return to his secret hideaway, although it would have been advantageous to listen to Frances's conversations, or to change clothes, but he decided to proceed with the final phase. Tonight, Ted would let Frances watch what he could do to *the most important person in the whole wide world to her*, and then maybe *she* would finally understand.

Chapter 55

FRANCES

Martin and I left the police station and hurried back to my apartment which was only a few blocks away. The decoy police officer sat on the floor hidden from view so it looked as if only Martin and I were in the apartment. The best-case scenario was that Ted would return to his hideout and this nightmare would end. If he was watching the apartment, he might return to his hidden room if nothing seemed out of the ordinary. The second scenario had Frances scared to death; not for her safety, but for Sophie.

The Alamosa police were finally able to hack into Sophie's laptop and open her email and Facebook accounts. She had no new postings on her Facebook, which was really unusual for Sophie; she usually posted her daily thoughts and agenda. The officers did hit the jackpot though when they accessed her email. There were the typical messages from friends, former colleagues, advertisements, but there was an email with *martinthehunter* in the *From* section and the word *Surprise* on the subject line. When they opened the email, they saw the instructions for Sophie's e-ticket to San Diego, confirmation number, and her strict itinerary for her surprise visit to Coronado to see her mom.

Now they had the upper hand and knew exactly where Sophie was and even when she had been seated for dinner. It was insane that they couldn't just go grab Sophie and whisk her away to a safe haven. But no one would be safe until Ted was caught and that was when I knew I had to make the toughest decision in my entire life; let the police use Sophie as bait.

The Coronado police sent some undercover officers into the hotel for surveillance and they had radioed back to headquarters that Sophie had been identified and was having a steak dinner with a glass of wine. Frances was glad that Sophie was oblivious to the danger she was in. The officers also reported that two men had separately approached Sophie, but she politely smiled, waved her left hand and shook her head. Neither man matched Ted's description or photograph. Sophie was a beautiful girl with a dynamite smile and I prayed I would see that smile again. The waiting was excruciating, but I knew that Ted had memorized my routine and could possibly be watching me even now, so I tried to remain calm.

For Martin's part, he was to leave the apartment and walk down Isabella Street to the corner liquor store at Tenth Street and Orange Avenue at 8:50 PM, make a purchase, and begin walking back to the apartment. That way, if Ted was observing their movements, everything would seem normal. I was to leave ten-minutes later and walk down E Avenue, cross the street to the beach entrance, down the sidewalk ramp past the restrooms and the lifeguard station, and then go left on the beach to the rock jetty, as per my usual nightly routine. The police were stationed strategically around the beach dressed as surfers, joggers, and even as a couple kissing on a beach blanket. Serving as the makeshift command center, the lifeguard post was manned, but the regular lifeguards had been sent home and two police officers were ready to light up the beach with the search lights used for night rescues.

The CBI had finally sent a couple agents to the Coronado police headquarters and were in the middle of bureaucratic red-tape to relieve the Coronado police of their involvement in the case and assume jurisdiction. The Coronado detective in charge knew that time was of utmost importance and felt confident that his officers had the situation under control. What could go wrong? They had all the bases covered and now they just had to wait for Ted to make his appearance.

CHAPTER 56

TED

Ted felt that the police were onto him, but wasn't sure if they knew about Sophie. After seeing Martin and Frances walk to her apartment from the police station, Ted felt the need to be overly cautious. He stayed clear of the parking garage and took back alleys heading toward the Hotel Del. He was still barefoot and he stopped in a passageway next to the dry-cleaners to pull out a shard of glass in his foot and he couldn't believe who he saw walking toward him, Martin. Staying in the shadows, Ted watched as Martin walked by and entered the liquor store—no surprise there.

He ran through the multitude of ways he could kill Marty-boy and then shove his redneck ass into the dumpster, but he did not have time to waste. Ted had a plan and could not be deterred from his mission, but oh how he'd like to slice Martin's throat. Ted continued down the side streets and alleys until he reached the employee parking lot of the Hotel Del. He used the cars as cover and made his way to a rarely-used entrance to the beach-front gardens of the hotel. Shirt and shoes were required inside the plush hotel, but it was commonplace to see guests, as well as beach visitors, walking around in cut-offs and no shoes outside so he would fit right in.

Ted snatched a towel and a hat that were lying on the rail of a first floor lanai and pulled the hat down tight and slipped the towel around his neck to try and conceal his face. There was also a baby stroller inside the railing three-rooms down so he borrowed it, too. He slumped over the stroller and hummed loudly so he didn't appear to be so tall or threatening. He just looked like a dad, or granddad, strolling with a baby around the gardens.

He found a bench at the edge of the ice rink where the lights were off until December when you could ice skate in the rink located close to the beach. The rink was a huge attraction for locals and tourists during the winter holidays—outdoor ice skating was only a stone's throw from the Pacific, and in seventy-degree weather.

No one walked by him and again Ted felt invisible even though he was pushing a baby stroller. At that moment, Ted realized that he had never pushed a baby carriage since he did not have children of his own, and then shook his head to vanquish the sad thought.

Ted then remembered seeing Martin at the liquor store and wondered if Frances would forego her routine visit to the beach for her nightly chat with God, and to say adieu to another day in paradise. Her routine was so predictable and he knew from hiding in the shadows exactly what her conversation entailed with God. What if Martin joined her on the beach and interfered with his plan? Only time would tell and Ted had spent way too much time planning the surprise to have anyone ruin it for him—Ted knew he should have sliced and diced Martin in the alley when he had the chance. He smiled at the graphic picture he had conjured up and then sat down on the bench to wait patiently for his date.

Chapter 57

SOPHIE

It was getting dark outside when Sophie wrote her room number on her check, G42, and smiled as she realized that forty-two was Martin's favorite number from when he played sports—this was definitely her lucky day. Leaving a tip for her waiter from her own cash, she put her wallet back in her purse and saw she had some messages on her phone, but didn't want to miss her mom on the beach so she would listen to them later.

Sophie was so relaxed after her spa treatment that she spaced-out her phone completely. As soon as the masseuse starting massaging her from the neck down, she forgot all her cares in the world. Knowing that Harlan and Brett were hunting, Martin was at the cabin, Taylor was at her granddad's house, and that her mom was off-limits, she really had no one else to call, maybe her Nana, but she didn't want her to know she came to San Diego without her.

She left the restaurant and walked down the outside steps to what seemed to be a maze of gardens and sidewalks that zigzagged down to the edge of the white sandy beach. She had walked by an area that looked like a huge dance floor; it had a railing around it that she thought might be used for wedding receptions. The gardens were beautiful and the smell of blooming flowers and salt water teased her senses. She wondered why more people weren't out enjoying this gorgeous night.

She saw only one other person in the gardens. He was sitting on a bench rolling a baby stroller back and forth—never even glancing her way. Sophie thought to herself how much more friendly people were in the small town her family had just moved to in Colorado, than the people here in Coronado. Oh well, she thought, I haven't lost it completely, there were two nice men that asked me to join them for a drink in the restaurant.

Taking a step onto the sand she decided to remove her shoes. Sophie turned to see if she could safely leave her shoes somewhere so she didn't have to carry them. Her eyes looked toward the bench where the man with the stroller had been. The stroller was still there, but he was nowhere in sight. Reaching the bench, Sophie's eyes traveled inside the stroller and saw that it was empty, except for a hat and beach towel. She shrugged and then placed her shoes by the side of the bench next to the white picket fence and hoped no one bothered them. She turned back toward the beach, checked her watch and then headed to the rock jetty as instructed by Martin to surprise her mom.

Chapter 58

FRANCES

Leaving the apartment, I followed my usual nightly routine and with trembling legs walked down to the beach. I am far from being a religious person, and surprisingly to those who know me, I do believe in God. I just refuse to believe that God is only there for people who sit inside a building, usually without windows, and pray to him on Sundays. God was about more than just being a good person on Sunday. I see myself as a good person, but many people judge me by my past and not who I am now.

I try to compensate for my colorful past by crocheting blankets for homeless babies and children, or blankets and hats for people battling cancer. I've donated time and money to the Special Olympics, the USO, and I always donate to our disabled veterans in honor of my grandma who volunteered over thirty-thousand hours to the local DAV chapter. My nightly visits to the beach rejuvenated my soul, gave me a chance to talk and pray to God, and I always thanked him for another beautiful day and night in paradise. Hopefully, he will be watching over Sophie and me tonight.

I walked slowly to my favorite location on the beach thinking how predictable I really am and said another quick prayer. I knew the police were close by, but still I felt so very alone. I understood why they didn't want Martin with me, but I could really use his strength right now. For the past fifteen-years he has been my *rock*.

I positioned myself in my customary spot, did my stretches, kicked at the waves a few times and did my best imitation of a yoga pose. I press my middle finger and thumb together and raise my arms up to the heavens and say, *Yahtahey*. It is an old Native American term Martin taught me that he liked from a classic John Wayne movie, *McClintock*. Martin said it means, "Greetings and good health my friend."

And so goes my nightly routine with God, the ocean, the beach and the invigorating waves buffeting the rocks of the jetty.

I just wish that I was writing this drama and could dictate the end to this madness. All of the innocent victims would still be alive and Sophie would be safe and sound. I would have Martin ride in on his horse and reach behind him for his rifle which was strapped to his back and blow a hole right through Ted's black heart. With that deadly thought, I hoped God couldn't read my mind, but asked for his help again, and trusted that he would end the drama his own way—as long as God's way kept my baby safe.

My thoughts drifted back to Sophie. A montage of pictures appeared before me. I saw my girl from the day she was born, with that little crooked-nose, through every year of her life until the picture in my mind was of the last time I saw her before I moved to Coronado. Then, emerging out of the darkness, I realized I was not imagining *this* picture of Sophie—Ted was cradling the limp body of my baby girl in his arms and was walking straight toward me.

CHAPTER 59

TED

Without even acknowledging her, Ted watched Sophie walk by him as he sat on the bench. She then took the sidewalk down to the sandy beach. He left the stroller by the bench, jumped the short picket fence, and hugged the outside of the pool house. From the shadows Ted waited for his prey.

The police on the beach spotted Sophie and then Ted, but without a clear shot they had to wait until Sophie was not in their line of fire. The undercover police had earlier cleared the pool area, and grounds of all the guests, and only Sophie and Ted were left in the outside gardens. Ted never realized that the baby stroller had saved his life because the police were not positive that the stroller was empty.

Ted's instincts alerted him that he was being watched. He had spotted all the police on the beach and also knew that the hotel's gardens and pool had been cleared of guests because it was now empty except for Sophie. Do police not understand that they give themselves away when they speak into their collars, cuffs or water bottles? He should train them how to become invisible. He knew by now there must be police tracking Sophie so he had to move swiftly.

In the darkness and hidden from view, he watched Sophie leave her shoes by the bench, turn and walk directly toward him. Slithering out of the shadows he revealed himself to the startled young woman who used to call him *dad*. With eyes wide as saucers, she gasped as she looked directly into his eyes. Then her knees buckled and Ted scooped her up before Sophie hit the ground. This was not part of his original plan, but neither was the police presence. Good thing the military trained him to think on his feet and be prepared for anything.

Holding Sophie in his arms, the police all froze on the beach. Ted knew the police were there, watching every move he made. He also realized that now *he* was in control because what mattered to them was Sophie's safety first and taking him down second. Game on boys.

Chapter 60

FRANCES

Ted slowly approached me; my feet were frozen in the warm sand. I screamed, "No! You bastard, what have you done to Sophie?"

He calmly said, "I caught her after she fainted."

The sound of his voice was eerily smooth and sweet; I couldn't believe my ears. Normally Ted's voice was intimidating and sounded like he was using a megaphone. What was happening? It all seemed so surreal. Why did all those innocent people have to die at the hands of Ted? If he wanted to hurt me, he had all the opportunity in the world to kill me, but here Ted stood holding my daughter's lifeless body and speaking so softly. It was then that I noticed the tattoos on Ted's arms, and felt nauseous when I saw a red heart with a jagged black line drawn down the middle that split my name in half on his right bicep.

At that moment, Sophie began to stir. I felt relief and with shaky legs moved closer. Ted jumped back and became the man I remembered. He forcefully stood a stunned Sophie up and firmly clasped his hands around her neck. Ted positioned himself behind her so no one could get a straight shot at him without endangering Sophie. He used her as a human shield—another skill I'm sure the military taught him. Sophie didn't say a word; she was terrified and was speechless. She did hold out her hand out so I could see that she was making the sign-language symbol for, *I love you*. Tears ran down my face as Ted began his diatribe.

Ted bellowed, "I found a Valentine you gave Sophie and you said you loved her more than anyone else in the whole wide world . . . what about *me* . . . you married *me*. You were supposed to love *me* more than anyone else in the world. I built you a dream home; took care of you and that's what I get? Then after I interrogated you about the Valentine you leave me and left me all alone. I always told you and Sophie that my hands were lethal weapons and I could kill people with my bare hands and I have. Did you ever connect the dots and understand how many people died because of *you*? You wrote mean things about *me* in your book and the blood of all those innocent people is on your hands. Young couples, who were madly in love, and I killed them so they wouldn't ever have to feel the pain of a broken heart. You broke my heart and now I will break your heart. I want you to witness the loss of someone you *love more than anyone else in this world,* and I want you to suffer Frances like I did when you . . ."

There was a sickening *thud* and Ted collapsed sideways into the surf edging the beach with Sophie still in his grasp. Ted's hands loosened around Sophie's throat and his body started to spasm. Blood began to pool by Ted's head—then just as quickly, the blood was dispersed with the ebbing tide.

My baby girl began crawling away from Ted and clawing at the sand to reach me. Hysterically crying, both Sophie and I sat in the sand and held each other tightly.

The police all converged on the scene and frantically asked each other who shot—no one had orders to shoot with Sophie still in harm's way. Then with guns drawn the police checked Ted's vitals and made sure he was dead, for real this time.

Martin raced down the beach from where he was positioned behind one of the recycle bins and slipped his cell phone back in his pocket. He fell to the beach and put his arms around his two girls.

With my heart racing and pounding loudly in my ears, I barely heard Sophie whisper, "Mommy, who shot Ted?"

Holding Sophie tight and shaking my head I said, "I don't know. It must have been an act of God."

EPILOGUE

A month after the deadly episode on the beach, police were still without a known shooter. The coroner determined that the bullet had entered the right side of Ted's skull and exited via his left temple. After checking all the Coronado police officer's weapons, it was determined that none of their weapons had been fired. Martin had been questioned and his hands checked for gunpowder residue and he was also cleared. Frances was in clear view of all the officers on the beach and she was also ruled-out as the shooter. The bullet would never be recovered, but was resting peacefully somewhere on the bottom of the ocean floor just west of Coronado beach.

It had been clear that Ted was set on killing Sophie. Whoever shot Ted was considered a hero in many people's eyes for saving Sophie's life and retribution for all the innocent victims. When all was said and done, Ted's savage mission included seventeen innocent victims, one man was seriously wounded, and one more dead if you counted Ted. The body of Ted's parent's neighbor had been discovered and from evidence left at the scene they could include his death as a murder and not a suicide as was once believed. The two young drivers that Ted spared, thanked their lucky stars when they found out what a monster they had given a ride to, and both swore to never give a ride to a stranger again.

Four Alamosa policemen and two campus police officers were given all expense-paid trips to Coronado, compliments of Mister L and the Missus, so they could meet their police counterparts. The Missus invited all the officers that were involved in solving the case over for an outside garden party to thank them for their services. Mister L was not there, he had a tee-time.

Sophie, Frances and Martin returned together to Colorado. Frances drove with her daughter to Alamosa to reunite Sophie with her family. Frances stayed a couple days and then met Martin at their cabin. For once they didn't work on the cabin, but relaxed, talked and made-up for lost time. After a month, Frances told Martin she was ready to return to Coronado, which was fine with him because he was getting ready for hunting season. They loved each other enough to let each other go, for now.

When Frances arrived back in Coronado, she checked her post office box and found a letter from her publisher informing her that there had been a surge in the demand for her first book of memoirs since Ted, in death, was now a cult figure. Her publisher said people wanted to read what she had written about Ted that would have triggered such rage and carnage. Frances hated knowing that she would make money off that monster and all those innocent people he murdered, so she decided that any money derived from the sale of her first book would go directly to the victim's families. She also received a belated birthday card signed by Nick, but the envelope had no return address or postmark—strange, and five-months after her birthday. Frances returned to her routine at the villa, but paradise would never be the same.

After Martin returned home, he also received an envelope with no postmark or a return address. The envelope was empty except for a small white business card with two typed underlined capital letters, T and E and one hand-printed underlined capital letter, D. Martin smiled and knew Nick was always one to get straight to the point. Although Martin hated to keep secrets from Frances, there was one he had to keep. Nick was not deployed in the Persian Gulf like everyone thought. After Seal Team Six shot and killed (Target Eliminated) Osama bin Laden, Nick entered the Navy Seal program and was stationed secretly on Coronado Island. The phone calls Martin made from outside the police department and again on the beach were to Nick's disposable cell phone. It gives a whole new meaning to, *don't ask, don't tell.*